Almost a Dead Ringer

Doreen Diller Humorous Mystery Trilogy, Volume 3

Margaret Lashley

Published by Margaret Lashley, 2023.

Copyright

For more information, write to: Zazzy Ideas, Inc. P.O. Box 1113, St. Petersburg, FL 33731

What Readers are Saying About Doreen Diller

"A great plot, exceptional storytelling and a whole new cast of fun characters make this one a must-read."

"What a delightful start to a new cozy mystery series by one of my favorite contemporary Southern authors!"

"Doreen Diller is pretty sure she didn't kill her boss. But, could the last few stressful days have turned her into a psycho-eyed homicidal maniac? Read it and find out!"

"I love books that grab me from the start, make me laugh and cry, and keep me glued to the end. This book is all that and more."

"Ms. Lashley takes loads of quirky characters, a twisty mystery, a pinch of romance, and a heaping helping of humor to create this masterpiece!"

"This book is hilarious. I couldn't believe how funny Doreen is. The craziness in this story was such fun to read. Doreen is my new favorite character."

More Mysteries by Margaret Lashley

Available on Amazon in Your Choice of Ebook, Paperback, Hardback & Audiobook:

Doreen Diller Mystery Trilogy (Three-Book Series)

https://www.amazon.com/gp/product/B0B2X3G3G7

Val Fremden Midlife Mysteries (Nine-Book Series)

https://www.amazon.com/gp/product/B07FK88WQ3

Absolute Zero (The Val Fremden Prequel)

https://www.amazon.com/dp/B06ZXYK776

Freaky Florida Investigations (Eight-Book Series)

https://www.amazon.com/gp/product/B07RL4G8GZ

Mind's Eye Investigators (Two-Book Series)

https://www.amazon.com/gp/product/B07ZR6NW2N

Prologue

Not long ago I, Doreen Diller, was a complete nobody.

Man, those were the good old days.

Ever take a trip inside the trunk of a Chevy Caprice? I don't recommend it. You see, three weeks ago, I played a crazy-eyed psycho killer on a low-budget TV serial. It aired on a Friday. By Monday morning, I'd already been called out as a murderer and hit over the head by an umbrella-wielding old woman.

The thing is, nobody told me that there's no escaping the public—or that in this digital age, no one seems to be able to tell the difference between entertainment and reality anymore.

I cannot overestimate how much this can totally screw up your life.

As an actress who failed to make it to the big screen in Hollywood, I don't know what being famous feels like. But being *infamous*? Well, it's like being stalked 24-7 by a clown carrying a mud pie with your name on it.

So if you've ever thought about becoming a serial killer—or even playing one on TV—take my advice.

Wear a really good disguise.

And don't let them use your real name.

Chapter One

The newspaper landed with a thump on the dining room table, right next to my bowl of Lucky Charms.

"Read it and weep," Aunt Edna said, shuffling past in her fuzzy slippers. She chuckled to herself as she took a seat across the table from me.

The paper was St. Pete's local tabloid, the *Beach Gazette.* My aunt had folded it to an article about Sophia's big party at the Coliseum downtown last night.

Twelve hours ago, the matriarch of the little-known southern branch of the mafia known as the Collard Green Cosa Nostra had turned 100 in style—if you considered narrowly escaping death to be stylish. And from what I'd learned so far about the gang of elderly mob ladies I was currently living with, I was pretty certain they *did.*

Sharing the same birthday as Sophia, I'd also turned a year older yesterday—only my odometer had clicked over to forty. I squinted at the newspaper. The only thing certain about my future was the need for bifocals ...

The article in the *Beach Gazette* was entitled, "*The Hundred Games.*" The headline was spot-on, considering Sophia's age and the underhanded shenanigans that had gone down last night. But it irked the stew out of me that the article's annoying author, Shirley Saurwein, had been clever enough to think of it.

The sarcastic, loud-mouthed, bleach-blonde reporter was quickly becoming my least favorite acquaintance *ever.* And as a gal who'd tried for 15 years to make it to the big screen in L.A., the list of scumbags I knew was longer than a trip up the Nile in a leaky canoe.

I scanned the newspaper article. Saurwein had made no mention of my heroic deeds in saving Sophia's life during last night's soiree. Or how I'd uncovered a scheming crook trying to defraud seniors of their life savings. Instead, Saurwein had decided to focus on clichés about

Florida's growing glut of "golden years" seniors with nothing but time on their hands and complaints in their mouths.

I had to hand it to her, though. The photo Saurwein had published to accompany her story drove home her point like a spear gun to the gut. She'd caught Sophia, our reining Godmother, glowering like an angry gargoyle at the two people cutting her centennial birthday cake.

The Queenpin's thin-lipped, Grinch-like scowl creased the lower half of her ancient, pasty face. Her catlike green eyes bulged with fury beneath the shiny silver turban she wore like a Jiffy Pop crown.

I pursed my lips. Sophia's tragic/comic visage reminded me of the absurd, bubble-headed aliens in *Mars Attacks*.

Well played, Saurwein. Well played.

I snickered, then caught myself. I glanced up at Aunt Edna.

"What's so funny?" she asked, peering at me over the rim of her coffee cup. A cultural relic from the 1970s, the only thing my aunt was missing were pink curlers in her hair.

"Nothing," I said, then set the paper down and picked up my spoon. "Well, at least it wasn't *me* caught in Saurwein's crosshairs this time. I think I might've made it through this whole 'turning forty thing' without any damage after all."

Aunt Edna raised a silvery eyebrow. "You sure about that?"

I frowned. "What do you mean?"

"Turn the paper over."

I did—and nearly choked to death on a mouthful of magically delicious cereal. Unfortunately, Saurwein's caustic article continued beyond the fold. The second part of it was punctuated by a photograph of me that was just as odd and unflattering as Sophia's.

I stared at the image of myself wearing Jackie Cooperelli's old-lady glaucoma sunglasses. I'd donned them to hide my spooky, pale-blue left eye from the public. But that wasn't what galled me about the photo.

During the party, I'd been stuck holding one of the guest's therapy animals—a grayish-green iguana the size of a wiener dog. Saurwein had captured the lizard and me both glowering into the camera like a pair of infuriated dimwits.

Even worse, my downturned mouth exactly mirrored the iguana's. The only difference was, *I* had lips. Well, at least more lips than that *lizard*, anyway.

Argh!

My grip tightened on the paper. I took a deep breath, then steeled myself as I read the caption Saurwein had written beneath the cringe-worthy photograph.

> *Younger hunger. Some seniors have forgotten how to age gracefully. Apparently, they're ready to do just about anything for attention—including, sadly, trying to look glamorous well beyond their expiration dates. Hitting a new low, accessories to attract attention now appear to include the exploitation of exotic pets.*

I gritted my teeth and hissed, "That woman is a menace to society!"

Aunt Edna smirked and shrugged her mannish shoulders. "Everybody's gotta have goals in life, Dorey."

My mouth fell open. As I waited for my brain to get with the program and spew forth a snarky retort, a different voice beat me to the punch.

"Morning, you two!" Jackie, Aunt Edna's ever cheerful sidekick, poked her pewter-haired head into the dining room. Wearing a flower-print shirt loud enough to bust an eardrum, she wagged her eyebrows playfully. "Brace yourselves, ladies. I've got the other birthday girl with me."

Jackie disappeared, then reappeared a moment later with Sophia on her arm. The rail-thin Godmother hobbled in, her silver turban slightly askew.

I snatched up the newspaper. "Did you see this?"

"Yes," Sophia said. She eased herself into a chair across the table from me. "Jackie. Coffee. Now."

"I'm on it," Jackie said. Springing into action like a soldier on a life-or-death mission, she scurried into the kitchen.

"What's so golden about the golden years?" Sophia muttered, picking lint from her black shawl. "My hair is silver and my butt's turned to lead."

My upper lip snarled. "At least *you* weren't upstaged by a freaking *iguana*."

Jackie returned with two mugs of coffee. She handed one to Sophia, then patted my shoulder. "Aww, Dorey. You got to learn to take things with a stain of salt."

"Jackie's right," Aunt Edna said, ignoring yet another classic Jackie malapropism. "Don't let sourpuss Saurwein get to you. She's just jealous. So, you ready to start your new job today?"

Jackie cocked her head at me and grinned. "Oh, yeah! You're taking care of Sophia from now on."

"*Her* taking care of *me*?" Sophia scoffed. "More like *I'll* be taking care of *her*." The ancient woman jutted her pointy chin toward me. Her thin lips curled slyly. "I'm going to make Doreen my pet project."

Aunt Edna leaned my way and whispered, "Better pray they're merciful at the kill shelter."

"So, young Doreen," Sophia said, eyeing me through her bejeweled bifocals. "Are you ready for lesson number one?"

"Um ... I can't right now," I said. "I have an audition this morning downtown. At Sunshine City Studios. If I miss it a third time, Kerri Middleton will have my head."

Sophia scowled. "And who says *I* won't if you go?"

"I do," Aunt Edna said. "Doreen made this lady Kerri a promise, Doňa Sophia. And we CGCN women keep our promises."

Sophia sighed. "Fine. When will you return?"

I shrugged. "I don't know. It depends on whether they want me for the part or not."

Aunt Edna smiled and raised her coffee cup. "Well, here's to hoping those studio folks give our Dorey here an offer she can't refuse."

"This ought to help even the odds," Jackie said, handing me a baseball bat.

"What's this for?" I asked.

Jackie beamed. "So's you can break a leg, kid. What else?"

Chapter Two

Achieving stardom in the acting biz was kind of like getting pregnant. Everybody was quick to congratulate you when you got the good news, but they had no idea how many times you'd gotten screwed before it finally happened.

Unfortunately, I'd yet to find real success as either an actress *or* as a girlfriend—much less somebody's mother. But this morning I was feeling pretty lucky just the same.

When I started out for my audition at Sunshine City Studios, The Toad, Jackie's ancient green Kia, had fired up on the first try. Usually the rusty green beast required a solid beating of its solenoid to get the engine to crank. But now, as I sat clutching the steering wheel, the car was shaking and purring like an asthmatic lion.

That had to be a good sign, right?

I smiled, shifted into reverse, and pulled away from Palm Court Cottages. Last night's performance—saving Sophia's life—had earned me six months free rent and all the linguini I could eat. I hoped my next performance at Sunshine City Studios would earn me enough to take care of the rest of my living expenses. If not, I'd have to start sewing my own clothes. Aunt Edna's pasta was going straight to my thighs.

Since I hadn't needed to apply "encouragement" to The Toad's solenoid, I was, for once, actually running ahead of schedule. I took this as yet another good sign—especially considering I'd been a no-show for my last two auditions with Kerri Middleton.

In all fairness, neither incident had actually been my fault. In both cases, my delinquency had been due to circumstances beyond my control.

The first time, I'd lost track of the hour while prying open a dead guy's jaws in a nursing home morgue. (Long story.) The second time? Well, let's just say I'd put the needs of the many above the needs of the few.

Me, of course, being the few.

But in the end, it had all worked out. While I'd been chasing down a murderer, the elderly former mob molls of the CGCN had managed to convince Kerri Middleton to give me a third chance at bat. In return, I'd promised Kerri I'd take whatever role Sunshine Studios had to offer.

For once in my life, things had ended in a win-win situation.

I smiled and hit the gas. Maybe my luck was finally turning around.

Chapter Three

I tugged nervously at the hem of my skirt as I picked my way down the cracked sidewalk along Central Avenue in downtown St. Petersburg, Florida.

Sunshine City Studios was in a red-brick building repurposed from an abandoned dry-goods store. It sat in the middle of an old-fashioned, main-street type section on Central Avenue. To either side of the studio were an eclectic mix of small, glass-storefront boutiques, trendy coffee shops, and tiny mom-n-pop diners.

Like me, St. Petersburg was in the throes of remaking itself. All around the old town, shiny, new high-rise condos were sprouting up like bamboo shoots. The towers appeared to be in competition with each other, vying to see which one could poke its head highest into the blue sky in hopes of affording its inhabitants a glimpse of nearby Tampa Bay.

The outward flashiness of the new "city residences" was in stark contrast to the dirty windows and grungy storefronts of their faded, aged neighbors—lingering reminders of how the city had been floundering just a short time ago.

As I nervously straightened the collar of my white silk dress shirt, the similarity to my own situation wasn't lost on me.

Since my mid-twenties I'd tried to make it as an actress in Los Angeles. I'd failed miserably. Then, after a decade and a half of doing the worst grunt-work imaginable, I'd finally caught a break. Like an angel from heaven, Kerri Middleton had called and offered me a role in a six-part, low-budget TV series called *Beer & Loathing* being filmed at the beach here in St. Petersburg.

Well, Kerri had *actually* only offered a role to soap-opera heartthrob Tad Longmire. Being his personal assistant at the time, I'd come along to cater to his every whim. How was I to know that fate would step in for me—and in the most unusual way imaginable?

As it turned out, I owed my big acting break to cheap rubber, dirt, and desperation.

• • • •

DURING FILMING *Beer & Loathing*, the original killer, an inflatable shark, had popped. With no budget or backup plan, production had slammed to a standstill.

While we'd all wracked our brains trying to figure out what to do next, wind had blown sand in my eye. I'd been forced to take out the contact lens I normally wore to hide my wonky pale eye.

Marshall Lazzaro, the young director on set, had caught a glimpse of my mismatched peepers. Out of time, money, and any better ideas, Marshall decided my "spooky cool" eyes would make me the perfect replacement psycho killer. He'd hired me on the spot.

I'd landed my first speaking part. But throughout filming, I'd had to hide behind a stupid rubber mask. And my voice had been electronically disguised. But hey, everybody had to start somewhere, right?

Unfortunately, it wasn't long before fickle fate had stepped in again—this time to ruin things for me. Right after filming wrapped on *Beer & Loathing*, someone stabbed Tad Longmire to death, *for real* this time.

With the star of the show suddenly "indisposed," the sixth and final episode had to be rewritten. Believe me, no one was more shocked than me when, in the final minutes of the very last episode, my unmasked face—and wonky eyes—were revealed as the mysterious psycho killer who'd stabbed Tad's character to death.

After that? Well, all heck had broken loose.

People from all over the place began calling the cops, reporting that I'd actually murdered Tad Longmire—*because they saw me do it on TV*.

Even though I was eventually cleared of all charges, some people's minds could not be unmade—not even, I suspected, some within my own new mob family. More than one of the GCGN molls considered me a "made woman." And the only way you get made in the mob was ... well, to whack, cut, pop, ice, clip, hit, burn, or put a contract out on somebody.

Anyway, like the city of St. Petersburg itself, I was now on the verge of putting my less-than-fabulous past behind me. Today, I was moving on with my life. I had a *real* audition. And this time, it was no twist of fate. I'd been chosen for my talent!

As I walked toward Sunshine City Studios, I was jittery with excitement. To calm myself, I took a deep breath and ran down my mental checklist.

Contact lens in to conceal my pale eye? Check.
No stains on my blouse, jacket, or pencil skirt? Check.
Hair and makeup intact? Check.

I marched up to the faded red door of the studio and knocked loudly, with confidence and purpose.

Move over, Mr. DeMille. I'm more *than ready for my close-up!*

As I waited for the door to open, I clicked my high-heels together for good luck.

Hey, it worked for Dorothy in *The Wizard of Oz*, didn't it?

Chapter Four

I was ready for my close-up, but apparently Mr. DeMille was not. Nobody answered the door at Sunshine City Studios.

My confidence deflating faster than a shot-down Chinese spy balloon, I reached up to knock on the door for a third time.

Had Kerri decided to stand me up this time, to get even? Was this whole audition just some perverse joke on me?

I bit my lower lip and pounded on the door. Suddenly, the door opened wide. A tall, slender, elegant woman in her mid-fifties beckoned me in with a graceful swoop of her hand.

"You're early," Kerri Middleton said. "I wasn't expecting that."

I winced. "Sorry. It's just—"

"Water under the bridge." Kerri winked a hazel eye at me and tucked a lock of silver hair behind her ear. "Here's to hoping three's the charm, eh?"

I sighed with relief. "Yes!" I grabbed her hand and shook it. "Thank you so much for giving me a third chance. I promise, whatever you need, I'm your gal!"

She grinned. "Good. I'm holding you to that. Shall we go and meet your new costar?"

I grinned. "Yes, of course! Do I know him or her?"

"You might. Follow me."

Kerri turned and marched down the hall, her heels clicking on the polished hardwood floor.

I followed her to the studio's familiar waiting room. It was a cozy sitting area furnished with a teal couch and two white leather chairs. I pictured Tad Longmire sitting languidly in one of them, looking bored and put out to have to be there.

I sucked in a deep, calming breath and thanked my lucky stars that my days of babysitting that spoiled man-child were over. Still, I wished it hadn't ended the way it did.

"Doreen?" Kerri asked.

I spun around to face her. "Sorry. Just lost in thought."

Kerri nodded as if she understood. "Doreen, I want you to meet Eddie Houser, your costar."

I glanced over at the paunchy, middle-aged man walking up to me and felt some of the starch go out of me.

"Nice to finally meet you," he said, reaching out a ruddy hand to shake mine.

"Thank you," I said, trying not to focus on the gold eyetooth gleaming inside his mouth.

The man grinned at me from beneath a black cowboy hat and a thick, wooly moustache that could've been lifted from the prop room of *Smokey & the Bandit*.

His face seemed hauntingly familiar.

But not in a good way.

Chapter Five

"Where have I seen you before?" I asked the man in the ten-gallon cowboy hat and fifty-cent moustache. "Wait. Did you play the father in *Joe Dirt*?"

The man laughed. "No. But thanks for the compliment. You probably saw me on TV, just like I saw you. Hey, where's that wonky eye of yours, psycho killer?"

I frowned. "Contact lens."

"Gotcha." He grinned and said, "Hey, watch this!"

To my surprise, he pulled a pair of finger guns from imaginary holsters on his hips, then popped off a couple of silent shots. "Figured out where you saw me yet?"

I smiled weakly. "Sorry, still not ringing a bell."

Kerri cleared her throat. "Doreen, let me introduce you to Eddie Houser of… Crazy Eddie's Used Cars."

Instantly, my mind swirled with images of old sedans, their windshields covered with painted-on prices that were riddled with fake bullet holes.

My mouth fell open. "You're the guy who's always shooting down high car prices."

"Ha!" Eddie laughed. "You got that right, little lady. And you're the weird-eyed killer who slashed Tad Longmire to death in *Beer & Loathing*!"

I crinkled my nose. "I didn't *actually* kill him, you know."

"Right." Eddie winked salaciously. "Between you and me, whether *you* did him in or it was somebody else, I'm glad Longmire's gone."

My eyes grew wide. "What? Why?"

"My wife had a crush on that ne'er-do-well rascal," Eddie said. "Around here, I'm used to being top dog. So, thanks for getting rid of my competition, so to speak."

"Huh?" I grunted.

Eddie slapped me on the back. "That's what gave me the idea to hire you in the first place. I figured if you could get rid of my rivals in *that* department, you could help me with my *business* competition, too."

I turned to Kerri, my eyes pleading. "What's he talking about?"

"I need a new shtick," Eddie said.

Kerri stifled a wince. "Um ... Mr. Houser is hoping to ... uh ... ride the wave of publicity from your role on *Beer & Loathing*."

"Get it?" Eddie said, slapping me on the back again. "*Ride* the wave?"

"No, I don't." I stepped out of slapping range. "What is it exactly that you want me to do?"

"Be my hired killer," Eddie said. "You and that wonky eye of yours. Bust it out, and lets you and me get busy slashing prices to the bone!"

I nearly swallowed my tonsils.

This must be how a bug feels when it hits the grille of a Mack truck.

I closed my eyes and tried to compose myself. Like that poor, hapless bug, there was no escaping what fate wrought for it, or for me. A promise was a promise.

Where's a Mack truck when you need one?

I opened my eyes, forced a smile at Eddie, and glanced over at Kerri. "Awesome. When do we start?"

Kerri winced again. "I'm afraid that, you know, since you missed your first two auditions, we're in kind of a time crunch."

My nose crinkled. "What do you mean?"

Eddie took a step toward me and put his hammy hand on my shoulder. "She means, little lady, that you need to get yourself all gussied up *right now*. We'll be shooting at my car lot on US 19 in half an hour."

••••

AS I STUMBLED OUT THE back door of Sunshine Studios, Kerri and Leslie, the young, blue-haired makeup girl I'd met filming *Beer & Loathing*, shoved me into a white van.

The van's engine was already running. At the wheel was Marshall, the young producer and owner of the studio.

"Good to see you Doreen," the handsome, 20-something blond man said. He grinned at me from behind aviator shades as I bounced onto the back seat with all the grace of a thrown garbage bag.

"Uh, you too," I managed to say as Leslie slid into the bench seat beside me, blocking my escape.

Kerri climbed into the front passenger seat and slammed the door. "Step on it!"

"You got it," Marshall said, and hit the gas. The van lurched forward.

"Am I being abducted, or what?" I asked.

"We're just in a time crunch," Kerri said. "And to be honest, business has been slow, Doreen. Not to mention we got stiffed by a couple of deadbeats. I know this isn't ideal, but we can't afford to lose this client."

I nodded. "Okay. I made you a promise. I'll do whatever it takes."

"Thank you." Kerri sighed with relief. "Now, let's get you prepped."

My nose crinkled. "Prepped?"

Leslie shoved a wardrobe bag into my lap. "Get into this outfit while I tease your hair."

I gulped. "Here? In the van?"

"It's either change in here or in the bathroom at Crazy Eddie's," Kerri said. "Trust me. The van is the choice you want to make."

I grimaced and zipped open the bag. "Um ... these jeans are a size six."

"That's what it said in your portfolio," Leslie said. "Five feet four, 115 pounds, size seven shoes, size six pants.

"Oh, sure." And I was—a month of eating Aunt Edna's pasta ago. "Here goes."

I stripped off my pencil skirt and heels. Then, trying not to grunt like a pig, I squeezed into a pair of jeans tighter than a tourniquet. Surviving that, I traded in my silk blouse for a Daisy Duke shoulder-less top.

"How do I look?" I asked, barely able to breathe.

Kerri turned and looked me up and down. "Better get out the filets, Leslie."

"The what?" I asked.

"On it." Leslie bent over and dug through her huge bag of props. "Here we go." She pulled out two pieces of flesh-colored rubber the size and shape of large chicken breasts. "Here. Stick these in your—"

"I know where they go," I said, snatching them from her hands. Begrudgingly, I shoved the rubber boobs into my bra.

"Eddie likes cleavage," Leslie said, then twisted her face in disgust. "Now, lean your head toward me so I can start teasing your hair."

Kerri shook her head. "Sorry, Doreen. The only thing Eddie likes better than big boobs is big hair."

I blew out a breath.

And the only thing I like less than playing a bimbo is clipping ugly old Arthur Dreacher's toenails.

Chapter Six

It had all happened so fast, it was still a blur. Or maybe it was just that those stupid jeans had cut off the circulation to my brain ...

"Come on," Leslie said, tugging me out of the van. "And watch the hair!"

I climbed out and caught a glimpse of myself in the van's side mirror. Blue eyeshadow glimmered all the way to my eyebrows. A fake mole loitered just above my lips, which had taken on the hue and shine of candied apples. My brown hair was the size of a beach ball.

"Who am I supposed to be?" I asked. "The leading lady in *Hairspray*?"

"Daisy the Price Slasher," Leslie said, handing me a rubber knife the length of a windshield wiper. "Remember, your motivation is to slash prices to the bone."

"Seriously?" At this point, my only motivation was to keep my personal dignity from meeting its own untimely death. But I had a sinking feeling that ship had already sailed.

"Come on," Leslie said, tugging me by the elbow. "We'll put the stilettos on you once we get you across the parking lot."

"Okay, okay!" I held my head high and followed her past rows of old, dented cars on their last legs. It certainly wasn't a glamourous gig. But the good news was, nobody could possibly recognize me in this ridiculous getup.

• • • •

IF IT WERE PHYSICALLY possible to die of embarrassment, I'd have never made it all the way over to the rusty blue Ford Escort parked in the middle of the lot at Crazy Eddie's Used Cars.

"Places, everybody," I heard Marshall yell as I tugged on the leopard-print high-heels.

"Nice," Eddie said as I fastened the buckles.

Creep!

When I stood up, Eddie's greasy smile evaporated. The shoes make me almost six inches taller than him, and he seemed none too pleased about it.

"Here, take this," Leslie said, handing me my rubber knife. "Now, stand next to Eddie by the windshield of the blue Escort."

I hobbled over to Eddie, feeling like a magician's bubble-headed assistant. I definitely needed rescuing from "the denim trousers of death."

"Ready, little lady?" Eddie asked, twitching his dime-store moustache.

I shot him a fake smile. "Ready as I'll ever be."

"Remember your lines?" Kerri asked.

I nodded. "Take that, you beastly prices."

"With a bit more enthusiasm?" she asked.

"I'm saving it for the real thing," I said.

"Fair enough." Kerri nodded at Marshall. "We're ready when you are."

"Okay, ready, set, action!" Marshall yelled.

Leslie slapped down the top of the clapboard. "Price Slasher, take one!"

I was surprised to see that Marshall was not only directing, he was manning the camera as well. Money must've really been tight, just like Kerri had said. Marshall zoomed in on Eddie as the used car salesman huckstered out his spiel.

"Howdy, folks!" Eddie tipped his black hat. "Now, when the little lady says she wants a new car, but you're short on cash, who you gonna call?" Eddie shrugged his shoulders and held his palms open wide. "Eddie Houser, that's who!"

"Bring your better half on over to Crazy Eddie's Used Cars. I'm sure we can make a deal. After all, I'm a sucker for a pretty face. Ain't that right, Daisy?"

"Oh, yes, Eddie!" I gushed, giving the camera a gander at my fake cleavage.

Eddie waggled his eyebrows. "So Daisy, how about you show the good folks out there how deep we slash those car prices?"

"You got it, handsome Eddie dear." I raised my rubber knife over the windshield of the dented, Ford Escort. "Take that, you beastly prices!"

Suddenly, I felt a hand grab my left butt cheek and squeeze.

"What the!" I gasped and swung around. As I did, the edge of my rubber blade skimmed across the neck of the fast-handed pervert.

"Argh!" Eddie bellowed. He grabbed his throat with both hands and stumbled backward.

"Oh, hell!" I screeched. "Mr. Houser! Are you all right?"

He looked up at me and grinned, causing his gold tooth to glint in the sun. "Ha ha!" he laughed. "I'm fine, darlin'. But I got you good, didn't I?"

"Cut!" Kerri yelled.

"No kidding," Marshall said.

I glowered at Eddie. "Excuse me, but you had no right to grab me like that!"

"Oh, come on," Eddie said. "I just wanted to get you to open up those crazy eyes of yours a little wider."

I scowled. "Believe me, my eyes are *wide open.*" I turned to Kerri. "I quit!"

I turned to go, but tripped on my stilettos. Kerri caught me by the elbow. "Please," she whispered in my ear. "You can't quit, Doreen. You promised."

I snorted steam through my nostrils. "Fine. But one more take and that's it. And if he grabs my butt again—"

"He won't," Kerri said. "I'll make sure of it."

"Awe, that's too bad," a woman's voice sounded from behind me. "I kinda liked it."

I whirled back around on my stilettos and nearly toppled over again. My mouth twisted into a snarl. "Shirley Saurwein! What the hell are *you* doing here?"

Saurwein laughed and twirled a lock of platinum blonde hair between her fingers "I was just driving by and happened to catch a glimpse of you coming out of that van."

She cracked her gum and nodding toward the Sunshine Studios vehicle. "I thought maybe you'd been kidnapped. Or is this a new look for you?"

"We're shooting a commercial," I grumbled. "This outfit is for my character."

"Oh yeah?" she quipped. "Who you supposed to be? Daisy Duke or Bride of Frankenstein?"

Chapter Seven

I slid into the backseat of the van, unfastened the button on my anaconda jeans, and gasped in a lungful of air. I rubbed the red ring encircling my waist. My face had to be just as crimson beneath the quarter-inch-thick layer of makeup it was smothering under.

"Geez, Kerri!" I grumbled as the van pulled out of the lot at Crazy Edie's Used Cars. "Daisy the Bimbo Price Slasher? Whatever happened to us making a difference for women with our film projects?"

Kerri cringed. "Sorry, Doreen. But sometimes you have to eat your vegetables first."

I blew out a breath. "I get that. But at this point, I'm beginning to think I'm doomed to be a lifelong vegetarian."

Kerri shot me a sympathetic smile. "Come on. It wasn't *that* bad, was it?"

My eyebrows met my teased hairline. "Not that bad? Whatever possessed you to think of *me* for this role anyway?"

"I didn't. Eddie Houser did. After seeing you on *Beer & Loathing*, he called me saying he'd pay a pretty penny to get you."

I sat back in my seat. "I sure hope he paid more than that."

Kerri grinned. "He did. But that's not the best part. Doreen, do you know what this means?"

I shot her a sour look. "That I have enough pennies to buy a veggie burger *and* fries?"

Kerri's nose crinkled. "No. I mean, well, yes. But it means something else, too."

"What?" I grumbled.

"It means you've got a *fan base*, Doreen. That's worth something, isn't it?"

I chewed my lip. "I guess. What's my take in this, anyway?"

Kerri smiled. "Five hundred dollars up front, plus five percent of all the extra profits for the next month."

"Studio profits?" I perked up. "That's really nice of you, Kerri. Thanks!"

"Not *our* profits," Kerri said. "Eddie's used-car sales profits. He's banking on a return on investment from his ads. It's his way of incentivizing you to want them to be successful, too. Pretty shrewd, eh?"

"For a lecherous dirtbag?" I groused. "Yeah, I guess. Anyway, at least it's all over with." I lifted my butt from the van's bench seat and started yanking off the merciless jeans.

Leslie grabbed my arm. "You can change when we get back."

"Are you kidding?" I balked. "I might not survive that long." I tugged the jeans halfway down my hips and scowled. "Why is it that we women have to do all this crap to try and be attractive, while men do pretty much *absolutely nothing*?"

Kerri bit her bottom lip. "I don't know. Sometimes I think we women do it to ourselves."

I peeled the legs of my painted-on jeans down to my knees and plopped my butt back onto the seat. "We're supposed to be perfect—not to mention *hairless*. Meanwhile, men walk around like bipedal apes. They don't even bother to cut their hair or shave their faces anymore!"

Kerri sighed. "That's one of the reasons I gave up dating." She shook her head. "We get what we put up with nowadays. And beards and cigars were the last two straws for me."

"You've got a point," Leslie said, swiping her blue bangs from her forehead. "See this? I got this new piercing on my eyebrow last week. My boyfriend Jeremy didn't even notice." She flopped back onto the bench seat beside me. "All he cares about is microbrews and his razor scooter. If I left him, I don't think he'd even notice until the beer in the fridge ran out."

"Hey, that's not fair," Marshall said, eyeing us from the rearview mirror.

"It's not?" Leslie said. "Prove me wrong."

Marshall winced. "Well, you know Jeremy better than I do."

"I sure do." Leslie glared at Marshall, then shot me a crooked purple eyebrow. "See? Told you."

I sighed and handed her the rumpled jeans. "Wouldn't it be awesome if the roles were reversed?"

"What do you mean?" Leslie asked.

"You know. That it was the *men* who had to be perfect, and all we women had to do was show up."

"Come on," Marshall said. "You women demand way too much attention from us. Anyway, Doreen, you should be getting plenty of it after this spot airs."

I grimaced.

Yeah. That's what I'm afraid of...

• • • •

AS I DROVE HOME IN The Toad, I glanced through the windshield and up at the sky, hoping a meteor would come hurtling down and put me and the Kia both out of our misery.

Who had I been kidding, thinking I was going to be offered a serious acting gig?

The Kia and I were both well past our prime. And just when I'd thought my acting career had sunk as low as it could go, I'd been forced to do the *bimbo limbo.*

I glanced in the rearview mirror at my makeup-free face, still ruddy from a good scrubbing in the Studio's bathroom sink. I cringed. Crow's feet were coming in for a landing around the corners of my eyes.

I blew out a breath. Whatever happened to the fresh-faced young woman full of piss and vinegar? The woman who'd been eager to fight the good fight against sexist portrayals of women in the media?

I know what happened.

I'd just traded her in for five hundred bucks and five percent of the profits on a lot full of dented Ford Escorts.

I scanned the sky through the windshield again. Still no meteor.

I hit the steering wheel with my fist and groaned.

"Argh!"

Not only had I kowtowed to the Hollywood clichés, I'd gone and forged new ground in objectifying women as weak-minded, simpering idiots.

And to top it off, that blasted Shirley Saurwein had seen me do it.

Chapter Eight

As I shifted the Kia into park in front of Palm Court Cottages, I envisioned the next edition of the *Beach Gazette* lying on the lawn.

In my mind's eye, the entire front page would be an image of me dressed as Daisy the "Bimbo" Price Slasher. The headline above it would scream out in big bold letters: *Doreen Diller, Still Unmarried and Unemployable at Age 40, Single-Handedly Slays the Feminist Movement.*

I groaned and I kicked open the car door.

"What's wrong?" Jackie asked, appearing out of nowhere. "Don't tell me somebody broke *your* leg!"

"What?" I grumbled, slamming the car door. Then I remembered she'd given me the baseball bat for luck. "Oh. No legs were broken. Just my spirit. And I broke that all by myself."

"Aww." Jackie slung a skinny arm across my shoulders. "Didn't go well? Don't you worry, kid. I know just the cure for that. A nice, steaming bowl of Edna's linguini Alfredo. Come with me."

I trailed behind the wiry, silver-haired woman like a child doomed for a dose of castor oil. As I trudged into Aunt Edna's apartment, I was surprised to discover the 1970s brown-and-avocado time capsule didn't smell like pasta sauce—or even Lemon Pledge, for that matter.

"Is Aunt Edna sick?" I asked.

"Nope." Jackie nodded toward the dining room. "Just busy. She's got her *own* job, you know."

"Really? I didn't know that."

"There's a lot you don't know about us yet," Jackie said as we entered the dining room.

Aunt Edna was standing beside the dining table talking on the wall phone—an ancient, dull-green landline with enough curly cord dangling from the handset to hog-tie three people.

"Call you back," my aunt said when she saw us, then quickly slammed the phone back into the cradle hanging on the wall. She grabbed a small notebook off the dining table and stuffed it into her apron pocket.

"Geez! What happened, Dorey?" my aunt asked as her eyes darted to the mop of teased hair atop my head. I'd tried to contain it with a scrunchy, but ended up looking like a fried Kewpie doll instead. "Don't tell me you got electrocuted!"

"No such luck," I said, flopping into a dining chair.

"Dorey's got the morbs," Jackie said. "I can tell by the infliction in her voice."

"In*flec*tion," Aunt Edna said, shooting Jackie a look.

"I told Doreen it's nothing your pasta Alfredo can fix," Jackie said.

Aunt Edna wiped her hands on her apron. "Well, it sure can't hurt. Let me fix you a plate."

"I'm not hungry," I said.

My aunt nearly tripped on her own feet. "What? You got a fever?"

"No, but I *am* burning mad." I crossed my arms over my chest and sulked. "Why is it that when a woman turns forty, she's considered washed up?"

Aunt Edna frowned. "Only in some circles, Dorey."

"Yeah," Jackie said. "Only the circles full of squares."

Aunt Edna started to scold Jackie, then stopped and cocked her head at me. "For once, Jackie's right. The only people who think 'women of a certain age' are has-beens are the ones too stupid to see beyond surface beauty. And you know what? In a way, it's a blessing."

"A blessing?" I scoffed. "What's so great about being over the hill?"

"Plenty." Aunt Edna put a hand on my shoulder. "I'm not saying you're past your prime, Dorey. But me and Jackie sure ain't gonna win any beauty contests no more."

Jackie beamed and elbowed my aunt. "You got *that* right, Edna."

Aunt Edna blew out a breath. "You don't gotta be *that* enthusiastic about it, Jackie."

"Enthusiastic about what?" I asked. "Being undesirable?"

Aunt Edna frowned. "I didn't say nothing about being undesirable."

I frowned. "Then what *are* you saying?"

Aunt Edna shrugged. "What I mean is, once beauty is off the table, everything else is wide open."

I cocked my head. "Huh?"

My aunt sat down in the chair beside me. "Some people have beauty for a while, Dorey. And some never have it. If you ask me, beauty is a burden. A curse, even."

I sat up in my chair. "I don't follow."

"Men know how to *work* beauty," Aunt Edna said. "They know how to manipulate you with it. But if you ain't got it, you ain't susceptible to their bull crap. In fact, you can turn the tables on them."

I studied my aunt. "What do you mean?"

Aunt Edna reached into her apron pocket and pulled out the notebook. She opened it to a page and shoved it at me. "See this list of guys, here?"

I glanced at the names of about a dozen men she'd written down. "Yeah. So what?"

Aunt Edna grinned slyly. "Every month, these guys send me money, hoping to hook up with me."

I nearly fell out of my chair. "What?"

Aunt Edna's face puckered. "Don't look so surprised. With the right incentive, any man can be yours for the taking."

Jackie winked. "You mean, 'any man can be taken.'"

"Same thing," my aunt said.

"Wait a minute," I said. "Are you having *sex* with these guys for *money*?"

Aunt Edna laughed. "No way!"

"She's more like their pen pal while they're in the pen," Jackie said. "Get it?"

"These guys are in j...jail?" I stuttered.

Aunt Edna laughed. "Yep. And these creeps ain't never getting out. Even if they did, they'll never find me. I have them send the money to a post office box downtown."

A weird mixture of horror and fascination and admiration and envy swirled inside me. "What do these guys get in return?"

"Something to brag to their cellmates about," Aunt Edna said.

"Let's just say Edna sends 'em a kiss to build a dream on," Jackie said.

I shook my head. "What are you talking about?"

Aunt Edna fanned through the pages of the notebook. A picture of a brunette bombshell in a one-piece bathing suit fell onto the table.

I snatched it up. "Whoa! Is that Elizabeth Taylor?"

"Nope." Aunt Edna beamed and pointed a thumb at her chest. "That's me, forty-eight years ago."

"You?" I gasped.

"Careful, Dorey." Aunt Edna showed me her palm. "If you say 'What happened?' I ain't gonna take it too well."

I shook my head. "No. What I meant was, I can't believe you sent them a *real picture of you*! Did you tell them your real name, too?"

"What kind of Reuben you think she is?" Jackie said. "Edna made up a name. It's a real doozy, too."

Aunt Edna wagged her eyebrows. "Liz Barker."

I eyed her skeptically. "How'd you pick that name?"

"On account of you ain't the only one who ever thought I looked like Elizabeth Taylor," Aunt Edna said.

"And Barker?" I asked.

"Because that was my mother's maiden name."

"Edna's grandmother was Arizona Donnie Barker," Jackie said.

My brow furrowed. "Who?"

Aunt Edna stared at me, slack jawed. "You playing with me, Dorey?"

"No. I swear."

My aunt frowned. "You really don't know?"

My eyes darted between the two women. "Know what?"

"Who Arizona Donnie Barker was," Jackie said.

I winced. "Um ... should I?"

Aunt Edna shook her head. "She was only the most famous female criminal in history."

"Oh." I smiled apologetically. "Sorry. Honestly, I've never heard of her."

"For crying out loud!" Aunt Edna moaned. "J. Edgar Hoover himself said she was 'the most vicious, dangerous, and resourceful criminal brain of the last decade.'"

"Give her a break, Edna," Jackie said, putting a hand on my aunt's shoulder. "That was a lot of decades ago."

Aunt Edna sighed. "I guess so. You know, in 1960, they even made a movie about my grandmother."

I grimaced. "I wasn't even *born* then."

My aunt hung her head. "Geez Louise. From America's most wanted to the dustbin of history." She elbowed her friend. "I guess we'll all end up there one day, hey Jackie? Some of us sooner than others."

I winced. "I'm really sorry, Aunt Edna."

My aunt locked her sad eyes with mine. "Dorey, my grandmother was Ma Barker, public enemy number one back in the 1930s."

My eyebrows shot up. "Hold on a second. Do you mean Ma Barker as in, *Ma Barker's Killer Brood*?"

Aunt Edna's lips hitched up into a tentative smile. "You've heard of the movie?"

"Heard of it?" I gasped. "I actually auditioned for the remake!"

Aunt Edna grinned. "No kidding!"

Jackie laughed. "What did I tell you, Edna? Dorey's got Barker blood running through her veins. Ha! You owe me fifty bucks."

"Can it," Aunt Edna grunted. "Dorey, you'd be perfect for the role. In fact, you kinda look like her."

"Uh ... thanks," I said. "So this dating service thing. You're actually stringing along a bunch of crooks for cash?"

Aunt Edna shrugged. "In a manner of speaking."

"How many have you got on the line?" I asked.

Jackie smirked. "A *Baker's* dozen. Get it?" She slapped me on the back. "Kinda ironical, considering Edna ain't had a date since she and Morty broke up."

Aunt Edna scowled. "Jackie, ain't it time for you to take some cyanide tablets or something?"

"Hold on." I turned to Jackie. "Are you in on this, too?"

"No way." Jackie laughed. "The way I see it, life is better without a man mucking things up."

I smirked. "You can say *that* again."

"Okay. Life is better without a—"

The phone rang. Aunt Edna jumped up, snatched the receiver from the wall, and pretended to club Jackie over the head with it. Then she spoke into the phone, pretty as punch.

"Hello? Oh, well yes, sir. Hmm. Let me see if she's available." Aunt Edna put her hand over the speaker and shot me a quizzical look. "Some guy asking questions about you."

I thought about Eddie Houser and grimaced. "Tell whoever it is, I'm not interested," I whispered, then winked at Jackie. "Like you said, I don't need some guy mucking up my life."

Aunt Edna nodded, and slid her hand from over the mouthpiece. "Sorry, Officer Brady, Dorey says she's not—"

"Hold on!" I yelped.

I sprang from the chair and snatched the phone from Aunt Edna's hand. The smug look on her face needed no translation.

"Careful," she whispered as I put the phone to my ear. "We wouldn't want some man mucking up your life now, would we?"

Chapter Nine

"What was that all about?" I heard Officer Gregory Brady ask as I held the receiver of Aunt Edna's old landline phone to my ear.

I picked at the flocked wallpaper on the dining room wall. "Don't ask."

He laughed. "Well, I certainly wouldn't want to muck up your life now, would I?"

I grimaced. "You heard that?"

"I did. Care to elaborate?"

I glanced over at Aunt Edna and Jackie. The pair were busy doing nothing as they loitered within earshot, eavesdropping in on every word Brady and I said to each other.

"Not at the moment," I said.

"The vultures circling, I take it?" Brady asked.

"Flap, flap."

Brady chuckled. "Here's an idea. Why don't you tell me all about it over an early dinner?"

I turned my back to the two elderly mob ladies and whispered, "Fine. As long as it's not that low-rent dive you took me to last time."

"The Dairy Hog?" Brady laughed. "Like I said, I wouldn't want to muck up your—"

"Stop!" I hissed. "Say another word, and you can forget about picking me up at six."

Brady must've taken me literally. His answer was a dial tone. I untangled myself from the curly phone cord and hung the receiver back on the wall.

"So, you two going out or what?" Jackie asked, pretending to dry a plate with a dishtowel.

I smirked. "Either that, or Aunt Edna didn't pay the phone bill."

"Huh?" my aunt grunted, snatching the plate from Jackie.

"Nothing." I sighed. "Look, it's been a long, strange day already, and it's barely past three o'clock. I'm going out for a walk to clear my head."

"Good idea," Aunt Edna said. "Just keep an eye out for Sophia. She's pretty eager to teach you a lesson."

I blanched. "What did *I* do?"

"Nothing," Jackie said. "You're her new assistant, remember? You gotta learn the ropes. And take my word for it. Sophia likes to give out just enough of it so's you can hang yourself."

My nose crinkled. "Thanks for the warning."

As I turned and took a step toward the front door, my aunt crossed herself, plucked the phone from the wall, and mumbled something under her breath.

It sounded like she said, "Mother Mary, have mercy on her soul."

• • • •

WITH ONLY A FEW HOURS before Brady was to pick me up, I didn't have the time or desire to get caught in Sophia's web. The way I saw it, that creep Eddie Houser had taught me enough lessons for one day.

With extreme caution, I stuck my head out of Aunt Edna's front door and peeked around. The coast was clear, so I headed outside and into the courtyard—a colorful jungle of palms, crotons, and plants I couldn't name.

The tropical courtyard was surrounded by five single-story detached apartments that made up Palm Court Cottages. The place was a little slice of old Florida, and was the exact opposite of my ugly, high-rise tract apartment back in L.A.

Eager to burn off some nervous energy with a walk, I snuck along the paved path toward the street, keeping an eye out for Sophia. I was almost to the street when my attention was suddenly drawn to faint grunts and groans coming from the azaleas beside one of the cottages.

What the heck?

I took a few steps closer. I could hear huffing and puffing. I spotted something pinkish-tan moving up and down in the azalea bushes.

You've got to be kidding me. All I need to top off this crap-shoot of a day is to spot a couple of wrinkly old love birds having a quickie in the dirt.

I grimaced, focused my eyes on the sidewalk, and picked up my pace. I was almost past the hedges when, all of a sudden, a head popped up from between the leaves. It belonged to an elderly woman. Her cheeks were as pink as the floppy hat atop her head.

"Kitty!" I gasped at the CGCN's resident gardener, scientist, and maker of sketchy potions. "What in the world are you doing behind the hedges?"

"Pulling weeds. What else?" Kitty grunted and worked her way up off her knees to standing. She gripped a garden spade in one hand, a drooping dandelion in the other. Her pink T-shirt read: *Botany Plants Lately?*

"How'd the audition go?" she asked.

I glanced down at the ground. "I don't want to talk about it."

"Oh. I see." She shot me a soft smile. "You should take up gardening, hon. You can't lose with gardening."

"What do you mean?"

"Just look at this monster!" Kitty held up the dead dandelion as if it were the prize catch of the day. At its leafy base protruded a taproot the size and shape of a white carrot.

"Uh ... nice one," I said.

"Isn't it?" Kitty grinned at me like Jack Nicholson in *The Shining*. "Ah! It's so satisfying to rip these buggers out by the roots. It's like pulling somebody's head off with the spine attached."

I stifled another grimace. "Right." My thoughts flashed back to how, last week, Kitty had made me hold open a dead guy's jaws so she could swab his throat.

Fun times ...

"Oh, look!" Kitty exclaimed.

I blanched. "What? Is there a dead guy in the bushes?"

"No. Even better!" Kitty used the dandelion's root to point at an azalea bush. "See there? It's a loveliness of ladybugs!"

My nose crinkled. "A loveliness?"

She beamed at me from under her pink visor. "That's what a group of ladybugs is called. You know, like a gaggle of geese? A pod of dolphins?"

"Oh." I leaned over and watched a "loveliness" of red, pill-shaped dots swarming around on the leaves.

"They eat aphids," Kitty said. "Suck the life right out of them."

"Nice to know."

"That's why they're red, I suppose. In nature, red means danger."

"And the spots?" I asked.

She shrugged. "Just a bit of bling, I guess. They *are* ladies, after all."

I frowned. "Not *you*, too."

She cocked her head. "What do you mean?"

"Never mind." I took a step toward the street. "I gotta go. I was just heading out for a walk."

"Catch you at dinner!" she called after me.

"Not tonight. I'm meeting with Brady."

Kitty beamed. "Oh, a date!"

"Not a date. A meeting."

"Well, in case you change your mind about that, I've got plenty of bling we can dress you up with!"

I forced a smile. "Thanks. I'll keep that in mind."

I turned and marched down the sidewalk, suddenly more nervous than I was perturbed.

Was it a date?

When it came to Brady, I was never sure.

Since I'd arrived in St. Petersburg less than a month ago, the handsome police officer had helped me out of two scrapes with the law—and had kissed me once in the moonlight.

All three times, I'd found myself completely out of my depth.

I chewed my lip and picked up my pace. Even so, I had the feeling that no matter how fast I went, there was no way I could outrun what lay in wait for me just around the corner.

Chapter Ten

I stared into the mirror hanging above the old, yellowing French Provincial bureau in my Aunt's spare bedroom—the one I now called home.

What should I wear to dinner with Brady?

Should I try to look attractive? Or should I try to look like I didn't try to look attractive?

I closed my eyes and shook my head.

Geez. Maybe Kerri's right. We women do *do this to ourselves.*

I'd come home from my walk as sweaty as if I'd been inside a Finnish sauna. Florida in June definitely wasn't for sissies.

A cold shower had cooled down my body, but not my heart. It was still racing in my chest. Was it pulsing wildly because I was going to see Brady soon? Or was it because I was still boiling mad over being duped into playing Daisy the Price Slasher?

I unwrapped the towel from around my wet hair and slathered on some conditioner. I hoped it had enough strength to undo Leslie's professional-strength tease-job.

Now, if only they made a lotion that could tame moods ...

I combed through my wet hair, glad to see it was beginning to relax, even if I couldn't. As I set the comb down, I spied my little yellow *Hollywood Survival Guide* lying next to the pink lava lamp.

"What sage advice do you have for me today?" I asked as I picked it up.

I closed my eyes, flipped through the pages blindly, and stopped at a random page. I opened my eyes to find that the *Guide*, like some Tinsel-Town Ouija Board, had landed on Tip #666.

> *Dress for the part you expect to play—unless, of course, you're expecting.*

The glib words hit me in the face like a clown's cream pie.

What role did *I want to play? Not just with Brady, but my whole life?*

As I stared blankly at the glowing globs of goo floating around in the lava lamp's mysterious pink liquid, a glimpse of something yellow reflected in the glass. I turned and saw the vase of yellow roses on the nightstand beside my bed. Brady had given them to me last night for my birthday.

I walked over to the bed and sat down next to the nightstand. Kitty had told me yesterday that yellow roses meant happiness, new beginnings, and friendship. If that message hadn't been ambiguous enough, Brady had also given Sophia an identical bunch.

What was I supposed to make of that?

I blew out a sigh. When it came to matters of the heart, I abhorred mixed signals. I'd had my fill of them from my mother, my ex boyfriends, and pretty much everyone I ever met in L.A.

I plucked a yellow rose from the vase and twirled it in my fingers. Hopefully, Brady would be straight up with me about his feelings tonight. If not, I was going to nip our yet-to-blossom romance right in the bud.

Chapter Eleven

I'd taken a chance on romance. I'd worn an off-the shoulders white blouse and snug—but not excruciating—jeans. Brady had looked pleased when he saw me. And I'd been just as pleased when he'd parked his black F-150 in the street next to Sundial, an open-air shopping and entertainment plaza in downtown St. Pete.

Brady had opened the truck door for me. He'd also led me up the escalator to the outdoor deck of an upscale seafood restaurant. When we were seated, he'd pulled out my chair for me. And when our waiter had appeared, Brady had taken charge, ordering a bottle of wine and a dozen raw oysters.

It was definitely a date.

••••

"AND THAT'S WHEN SHE told me her grandmother was Ma Barker," I gushed to Brady, feeling giddy after a glass of red wine and a couple of oysters.

"Seriously?" Brady asked. His handsome smile faded a notch. "*The* Ma Barker?"

I nodded. "Yes. The very same. You don't believe me?"

"It's not that." Brady set his glass of wine on the table and smirked. "Just keep in mind, Doreen. This is the same woman who told me she saw Mongo the Monkey Boy on TV."

I choked on a sip of wine. "What?"

"While I was waiting for you to get ready, your aunt told me she'd seen a guy she used to know on the Channel 22 news." Brady shook his head. "I figured she had to be joking. I mean, who would have a nickname like Mongo the Monkey Boy?"

I thought about some of the other people my aunt and her friends hung around. Victor "the Vulture" Ventura, who could make bodies disappear. Victoria "Slick" Polaski, the red-headed bombshell who'd claimed to be Freddy Sanderling's fiancé at his funeral. And, of course, Sammy the Psycho, Sophia's psycho killer son with a penchant for cheese curds.

I shrugged and smiled at Brady. "Gee, I really couldn't say."

He waggled an eyebrow at me. "Couldn't? Or won't?"

I played dumb. "I've never heard of this monkey boy, I swear. Maybe he's one of my aunt's boyfriends."

Brady's eyebrow went still. "One? How many does she have?"

I laughed. "About a dozen. Just old-school, snail-mail romances. But they're not real."

"What do you mean?"

"You know," I said, twirling a lock of brown hair in my fingers. "They exchange letters, but they never actually meet."

Brady's casual demeanor took on a more serious tone. "Why would they never meet?"

"Uh ..." I shifted my gaze to my wine glass.

Crap. I've said too much. Dang it, cabernet!

"Well," I fumbled, nervously tapping a finger on my wine glass. "On account of ... it could be because the men are ... uh ..."

"Incarcerated?" Brady asked.

I cringed and looked up at him. "Maybe."

Brady shook his head. "Poor Edna. Do you know if these guys are bilking her for money?"

I glowered at myself for ratting out Aunt Edna. Then realized Brady had it all wrong. It was more like the other way around.

"I don't know," I said. Which, technically, wasn't a lie.

Brady's brow furrowed. "Doreen, your aunt could be the victim of a lonely hearts scam."

"Really?" I pretended to gasp. "Is that illegal?"

"Yes. Last time I checked. I need to talk to her about it."

"No. Let me," I blurted. "She might be ... you know ... embarrassed. We women have our pride."

"But she could—"

"I tell you what," I said. "I'll ask my aunt if these guys are trying to get money from her. I promise I'll let you know if she's been duped and wants to press charges, okay?"

"Okay." Brady shook his head softly. "It's a crime, you know."

"This lonely hearts club band thing?" I asked.

"No. I mean, yes. But that wasn't what I was referring to. I meant it's a crime what love does to people. It makes them do crazy, desperate things."

I shot Brady my best doe eyes. "Are you speaking from experience?"

Brady pursed his lips. "Listen, Doreen. I didn't want to get together with you to talk about your aunt."

I smiled coyly. "You didn't?"

"No. I wanted us to meet so we could discuss what went down at Sophia's party last night."

"Oh."

My racing heart slammed on the brakes. "Was that only last night?" I asked, trying to hide my disappointment. "It seems like that happened ages ago. I guess times flies when you're not having fun."

"What?" Brady asked, busy pulling a notepad from his shirt pocket.

"Nothing." I reached for my wineglass and drained it. As I set it back on the table, I noticed Brady was smiling at me.

"You really did amaze me," he said.

I stifled a belch. "I did?"

"Yes. The way you figured out that it was Melanie who trying to con those old folks at Shady Respite out of their life savings. And then you go and top it off by foiling her plan to poison Sophia. That's like hitting a double header, Doreen!"

"Thanks."

Nothing like a sports analogy to win a woman's heart...

Brady laughed. "You're a real prize fighter. The way you kept coming back for more, even after Melanie shot you down over and over again for making false claims and amateur mistakes—"

I frowned and refilled my wine glass. "Is there a point to all this?"

Brady cocked his head. "I thought I just made it. It's *you* who gets the credit for figuring out the case."

I shrugged. "Thanks. But I already knew that. So, is that why you wanted to see me?"

Brady nodded. "Yes. I figured I at least owed you dinner for that."

Great.

I raised my wine glass. "Well, consider the debt paid. And thanks again for the yellow roses you gave me and Sophia."

"Another token of my appreciation." Brady clinked his glass against mine. "Your work broke the case. Now mine is just getting started."

"What do you mean?" I asked, then gulped my wine and imagined beating him over the head with a bunch of yellow roses.

Brady grinned. "I'm the one who has to wade through the mountains of paperwork. I've been working on the case since seven this morning."

"Sorry to ruin your day," I said sourly.

Brady's brow furrowed. "I didn't mean it that way."

I stabbed an oyster with a little fork. "What way *did* you mean it?"

"What I meant is that I'm proud of you, Doreen. You're a one-woman *tour de force*. After interviewing Montoya, I—"

"Montoya?" I asked.

"Melanie Montoya. That's the con-woman's name—her *real* one, that is. I went through her personal effects and found four different IDs with her picture on them. And that notebook she had? It contained signed powers of attorney from at least a dozen other elderly victims she was planning on duping into giving her control of their assets."

I grimaced. "That many?"

Brady nodded. "That may be just the tip of the iceberg." He shook his head. "What kind of cold heart takes advantage of people in nursing homes who have no one around to stick up for them?"

"The same kind that uses innocent animals to sneak into their hearts—then into their wallets."

Brady nodded solemnly.

I gulped half a glass of wine for courage, then began my own line of questioning—about where our relationship was headed.

"Speaking of hearts ..." I said.

But Brady wasn't listening. He was staring off into space, probably consumed with thoughts about the next sporting reference he could "compliment" me with.

Annoyed, I let the rest of my question drift off, just as his attention had. Apparently, I wasn't as interesting to him as football, or Melanie Montoya, the heartless scammer.

Speaking of heartless ...

I shook my head and studied the handsome cop sitting across from me. Brady was about the same age as me. In society's view, he was a man in the prime of his life. I, on the other hand, was well past *my* prime. As the world saw it, my worth was unraveling faster than a Walmart sweater.

Life is so unfair.

"More wine?" the waiter asked, startling both me and Brady out of our unshared daydreams.

"Yes, please," I said.

"Not for me." Brady put a hand over his glass. "I'm driving."

The waiter drained the last of the bottle into my glass. I snatched it up.

"I was just thinking—" Brady said.

"Let me guess," I interrupted. "About baseball, or the case?"

"The case." He shook his head. "I'm not convinced Montoya could've pulled all this off on her own."

"I agree," I said, reluctantly.

Brady looked surprised. "You do? Why?"

"Because she doesn't have a cleft chin." I slugged back more wine.

Brady's brow furrowed. "Excuse me?"

I sighed. "Sophia told me the person who delivered the poisoned lemon bars to her room at Shady Respite had a cleft chin."

Brady nodded. "Right. But couldn't they've just been a hired delivery person?"

"I guess. But somebody had to let this delivery person into the nursing home after visiting hours."

"Unless they worked there." Brady leaned back and drummed his fingers on the table. "Or they could've arrived earlier, hid out, and waited until the coast was clear to deliver the cookies."

I shot him a sour, tipsy smile. "You're really good at shooting down my ideas. Are you like, a trained sniper or something?"

Brady laughed. "No. It's just the way we work here at the station."

I slammed my wine glass on the table and crossed my arms over my chest. "In case you haven't noticed, we're not 'here at the station,' Brady."

He locked eyes with me. "I'm not trying to prove you wrong, Doreen. I'm only trying to look at all the plausible explanations."

I blew out a breath. "Yeah. I know."

I only wish that one of those plausible explanations was that we were here because you fancied me.

"Let's say this delivery person was in on it," Brady said, oblivious to my plight. "Do you have any ideas as to who it might be?"

I gave up my lost cause. For Brady, this was a business meeting, nothing more. "Yes," I said. "It's probably a guy."

"Why do you say that?"

I swallowed the knot of anger in my throat. "Sophia said whoever it was had a deep voice, and used a pompous, high-brow tone. I thought it might've been Neil Neil from Neil Mansion funeral home, but he doesn't have a cleft chin. Neither does his partner."

Brady nodded. "So, who does?"

"Have a cleft chin?" I asked.

"Yes."

"A lot of people. In fact, approximately 25.9% of the population. Cleft chins are the most common in people with European, Middle Eastern, and Southern Asian ancestry."

Brady raised an eyebrow. "Sounds like you've been doing some homework."

I shrugged, feeling a bit woozy. "A little."

"Anybody fit this bill that I should be aware of?

I hiccupped and leaned in toward him. "Yes. Humpty Dumpty. I mean Humphrey—"

Brady burst out laughing. "Good one, Doreen." He shook his head and grinned. "You really had me going there for a minute. Let me guess. Is this Humpty Dumpty guy the father of Mongo the Monkey Boy?"

Oh no he didn't!

My last nerve snapped. Brady had chosen the wrong day to make me the butt of yet another man's joke.

"How would I know?" I hissed at him. "Why don't you ask my Aunt Edna?"

Brady picked up his wine glass and winked at me. "Well, like you said, I wouldn't want to embarrass her."

I glared at him like an angry mother bear. "Is that all you needed from me? If so, I want to get out of here."

Brady's goofy grin vanished. "What about dinner?"

"Now!" I said, and banged my fist on the table.

"Um ... sure. If that's what you want."

I scowled. "It is."

"Okay. Wait here. I'll get the check."

As soon as Brady left, I slugged down the rest of my wine and glared at all the stupid, happy couples walking around hand-in-hand in the courtyard below.

I chided myself. What a fool I'd been to think Brady would consider me girlfriend material.

Suck it up, Doreen. You've made it this far on your own. You don't need Brady, or anyone else for that matter. The only person you can depend on in this world is yourself.

I spotted Brady's truck parked along the street and dreaded the tension-filled ride home that awaited me. As people strolled by the F-150, I noticed one had stopped and was now staring up at me. I tried to make out his or her face, but the hoodie they wore shaded their eyes and nose.

As I stared down at distant figure, the person held up something shiny. He or she thrust it toward me, then turned and disappeared into the crowd. Whatever had been in their hand had glinted in the streetlamp light like a knife blade.

And whoever it was, man or woman, had a distinctive cleft chin.

"You ready?" Brady asked.

Startled, I gasped and whipped around to face him.

"What's wrong?" Brady asked.

"Nothing!" I scrambled up from my chair. "Nothing you need bother to take seriously, at any rate. Let's go."

Chapter Twelve

I sat up in bed and nearly screamed. My pajamas were stained with blood! Then I realized it wasn't blood. And I wasn't wearing pajamas. I was still wearing the white shirt from last night. And it was splattered with wine.

I nearly gasped.

Last night!

There wasn't enough red wine in the world to erase the memories of the catastrophe that would forever be emblazoned in my memory banks as "The Sundial Disaster."

I blew out a breath and wondered, was it just me? Or was it normal for a woman's world to implode the moment she turned forty? After all, that's what Hollywood films always told us would happen.

Even so, the word "implode" didn't do justice to the 24 hours I'd experienced since turning the big four-oh.

For starters, I'd been upstaged by an iguana in the daily news. Then I'd nearly been cut in half by a pair of jeans. My hair had been teased to within an inch of its life. Crazy Eddie Houser had grabbed my ass. And I'd humiliating myself along with all of womankind by playing Daisy the bimbo used-car price slasher.

But that had just been Act One.

Act Two had been my disastrous date with Brady.

He'd probably never talk to me again.

I rubbed my pounding forehead and tried not to think about it. But I couldn't help myself. The memories from last night kept surging back like a bad case of acid reflux.

• • • •

INSTEAD OF HAVING BRADY take me straight home, I'd insisted he drop me off at a convenience store a few blocks from Palm Court

Cottages. He'd wanted to accompany me inside, but I'd gone and pulled the FCP-card. I'd told Brady I'd needed to buy some feminine care products—and I wanted to do it alone.

As I'd climbed out of his truck, I'd practically begged Brady to leave. I'd argued that I'd be fine walking home by myself. (I'd planned to arm myself with a huge bottle of wine.) But as I'd sorted through the alcohol on offer in the store, I could see Brady waiting patiently for me in the parking lot.

Brady's "chivalry" had forced me to change my plans. Instead of buying a decent bottle of cabernet, I'd had to resort to purchasing a cheap box of wine the shape of a family-sized carton of tampons. In hindsight, I suppose Brady had done me a favor—I'd planned to guzzle the wine, and it was a lot harder to chip a tooth on cardboard than on glass.

Anyway, after I'd left the store, Brady and I'd exchanged a few words in the parking lot. Exactly, which words I couldn't recall. I only remembered that I'd refused to get in the truck with him. Eventually, he'd given up and let me have my way.

A vague recollection made me cringe.

Had I kicked his truck as he'd pulled away?

I blew out a tired sigh, then leaned across the bed and dragged my laptop to my side. The movement set off a base drum pounding inside my skull. I groaned, then powered up the computer and opened a search browser.

According to Google, the odds of winning the PowerBall lottery were one in 195 million. Meanwhile, the odds of being struck by a meteorite were nearly 800 times higher, at 250,000 to one.

I snapped the computer shut. With neither my salvation nor my demise as eminent as I'd hoped, I resigned myself to slogging through another day.

I pinched the bridge of my nose in an attempt to ease my aching head. It didn't work. I put aside the computer and fumbled for the leather-bound journal on my nightstand. The beautiful notebook had been a birthday gift from Kitty. She'd encouraged me to write down my observations in the journal. Kitty thought I had a knack for "seeing the big picture."

I'd definitely proved her wrong yesterday.

I sighed and opened the journal to the first page. The night before last, I'd scrawled a note on it, right after my own little birthday celebration was over.

Humpty Bogart has a cleft chin.

I rummaged around in the nightstand drawer for a pen. I had a few choice observations about turning forty I wanted to jot down. As my fingers wrapped around an ink pen, a knock sounded on my bedroom door.

"Up and at 'em, Dorey," Aunt Edna's voice rang out. "Coffee's ready, and so is Sophia."

I slumped back onto the pillows.

Oh, crap. I'd forgotten all about Sophia.

• • • •

I PULLED A COFFEE MUG from my aunt's kitchen cupboard. The inscription on it read:

Good morning. I see the assassins have failed.

I shook my head and muttered, "Man, I can't catch a break."

"What's that?" Jackie asked strolling into the kitchen. Dressed in a screaming yellow shirt and matching pants, she looked like an overgrown banana Popsicle.

"Nothing," I said, shielding my eyes from the glare of her clothing. I filled my mug with coffee. "Did you see the paper this morning?"

"Which one?" Jackie asked.

"The *Beach Gazette*."

"Nope. It only comes on Wednesdays and Saturdays, kiddo."

"Oh. Thanks."

Bleary-eyed, I did the math in my head. Today was Thursday. Crazy Eddie's ads didn't start airing until tomorrow. And thanks to Jackie, I now knew the progeny of Saurwein's poison pen couldn't possibly go to print until Saturday. That meant I still had around 24 to 48 hours before the rest of my life turned into complete dumpster juice.

"Big day, eh?" Jackie asked as I passed the carafe of coffee to her.

"What do you mean?"

"Your first day as Sophia's new assistant."

I winced.

Make that 24 to 48 seconds *until my life hit Dumpsterville.*

"Don't remind me," I said, grabbing a box of Lucky Charms from atop the fridge. The sight of the grinning leprechaun on the box only curdled my already sour mood.

Lucky Charms? Since when?

I shoved the cereal box back on top of the fridge and took a giant slurp of coffee.

"You're gonna need your strength," Jackie said. "Top off your cup?"

"Please."

Jackie filled my assassin cup, then I dutifully followed her glowing yellow pantsuit into the dining room.

"Morning," Aunt Edna said as Jackie and I took our places at the table next to her and Sophia. I noticed that, besides her silver turban, the ancient Queenpin was dressed all in black.

"Morning, Sophia," I quipped. "Whose funeral is it?"

Sophia's green cat eyes narrowed in on me. "I don't know. I haven't decided yet."

I glanced over at Aunt Edna. She smirked at me from behind the rim of her coffee cup. "Time to earn your keep around here, Dorey. There ain't no such thing as a free lunch, you know."

"Don't you mean free breakfast?" Jackie asked.

"It's a figure of speech," Sophia grumbled, then turned and studied me. "So, young Doreen. Are you ready for lesson number one?"

I smiled weakly. "Sure. Let me go put on my flip-flops and I'm all yours for the day."

• • • •

AFTER SCROUNGING MY pink rubber sandals from the closet, I turned around to find Aunt Edna standing over me.

"What's up?" I asked.

"Just wanted to tell you not to worry, Dorey."

"Worry?" I asked, suddenly full of dread. "Should I be worried?"

"No." She patted me on the back. "You're gonna be fine. Sophia can be tough, but remember, you come from a long line of mobsters who were even tougher."

I frowned. "You mean like Mongo the Monkey Boy?"

Aunt Edna's face went pale. "You know about Monkey-Faced Mongo?"

"Sure. He was on the Channel 22 news, right?"

"Yeah." Aunt Edna grimaced and rubbed her palms on her apron. "He's one of my uh ... pen pals, Dorey. He ... uh, got out of prison a couple of days ago."

"What?" I gasped. "I thought you said those guys would never get out."

"Not legally," Aunt Edna said. "He ... escaped."

I took my aunt's hand. "But he ... he can't *find you*, right?"

Aunt Edna winced.

"Right?" I asked again.

"Doreen!" Jackie yelled from another room.

Aunt Edna's eyes grew wide. "Don't tell Sophia about ... you know."

"The lonely hearts scam you're running?" I said, inching my feet into the pink flip flops.

Aunt Edna's worry lines softened. "Yeah. Not a peep, okay?"

Jackie burst into the room and grabbed me by the arm. "Come on, Dorey. We gotta go. Now!"

"What's the rush?" I asked.

"Sophia needs to get back to her place. Her bladder ain't what it used to be."

Aunt Edna shook her head and sighed. "Neither is mine."

Chapter Thirteen

"Take it easy, I'm not a racehorse," Sophia grumbled as I helped her along the path to her apartment.

"Why don't you use that fancy wheelchair of yours?" I asked, tightening my grip on her elbow.

"And look like a weakling?" She tugged at the black shawl draped over her shoulders, even though it was nearly ninety degrees outside. "Besides, my hip is fine."

"Is that because the fracture healed, or because you never had one to begin with?" I quipped.

"That's my private business, young lady," Sophia snarled. "And you'd be wise to keep clear of it."

I grimaced. "Yes, ma'am."

"Getting old sucks," Sophia muttered as she unlocked the door to her cottage and slowly stepped inside. "My shoulders are always freezing and my feet are hot as coals." She hung her shawl on a hook on the wall, then hobbled over to the couch and flopped into it.

"I thought you had to go to the bathroom," I said.

"I told Jackie that so I could escape her idiotic jokes."

My eyebrow rose a notch. "Well played. So, where do we start? With the mafia lessons, I mean."

"Eager," Sophia said, eyeing me up and down. "I like that. Well, we start with lesson *numero uno*, of course. 'The Family always comes first.'" She smiled at me. "But you already proved that at my party the other night."

"I did?" I asked.

Sophia picked up the TV remote. "You saved my life from that fruit fly with the iguana. I remember the lizard's name. Iggy. But what was hers?"

"Melanie Montoya. At least, that's what Brady told me last night." I winced at the thought of our meeting gone awry. "Brady said Montoya had a bunch of fake IDs on her. And a stack of power of attorney forms with scammed signatures on them."

Sophia nodded. "Not a bad scheme, actually. That hustler would probably be a fat cat if she didn't eat alone."

"Eat alone?" I asked.

"Get greedy." Sophia clicked the TV on. "If this dame had shared a piece of her action with the Family, she might still be in business. With a scam like that, you need backup."

"So you don't think she ran the con all by herself?"

"Nah. She had the charisma, but not the brains."

I chewed my bottom lip. "That's what I was thinking, too."

Sophia shrugged. "Eh, what does it matter now? She got pinched. The cops caught themselves a fish. No need for them to keep baiting the hook anymore, is there?"

"But if someone else was involved, shouldn't we—"

"Excuse me, Doreen. You forget what side of the fence you're on? You're a member of the Collard Green Cosa Nostra, not the St. Petersburg police force."

"I know. It's just that—"

"Basta! Enough already! Do you need to relearn lesson number one?"

I pursed my lips. "No ma'am. The Family always comes first."

"Good. Now, time for lesson number two. 'Cleanliness is next to godmotherliness.'"

I cocked my head. "Excuse me?"

Sophia threw her arm in the air. "Clean up this place!"

I blanched. "What?"

"Get to it. You can start by taking out the trash."

"Sorry. Is that a euphemism for—"

Sophia shook her head. "Geez. The can in under the kitchen sink cupboard, already."

"Oh. Right."

I walked into the kitchen and took the lid off the trash can. To my surprise, it was full of paper Starbucks coffee cups. I pulled out the liner and placed a clean one in the can. Then I toted the dirty bag into the living room, where Sophia was busy watching *Wheel of Fortune*.

I held up the sack. "I take it Aunt Edna still doesn't know you're drinking Starbucks coffee instead of hers?"

"That's not Starbucks," Sophia said. "It's ScarBux. The new place down the street. They got free delivery, too. The guy's here like clockwork every morning at 5:30."

My right eyebrow ticked upward. "You let the delivery guy in here every morning? Isn't that dangerous?"

"No more deadly than drinking Edna's awful coffee. Pure battery acid. You could dissolve a body with it."

I frowned. "I don't mind it."

Sophia looked down at me through her bifocals. "You might when your body's a hundred years old."

"Fair enough."

"Tell you what, young Doreen. Since you're so worried about my health, from now on, you can be here at 5:30 every morning to meet the delivery guy and pay him for the coffee. How's that sound?"

It sounds like a trap I just laid for myself, that's what.

• • • •

WHILE SOPHIA SHOUTED out possible solutions to *Wheel of Fortune* puzzles, I washed the dishes and herded up enough dust bunnies from under her bed to fill another trash bag. Apparently, Aunt Edna didn't have the same standards of cleanliness for Sophia's place that she had for her own.

I wonder what the mob word is for slacker?

I poked my head into the living room. A commercial was playing on the TV. While Sophia sipped coffee and waited for Pat and Vanna to return to the screen, I seized the opportunity to ask her a question.

"Sophia? I was wondering if you could teach me more mob lingo."

She shot me a dubious look and straightened her turban. "What are you talking about?"

"You know. Like how 'eating out' means greedy. I already know that lemon bars mean money. And money runners like Humpty Bogart and Vinny Zamboni are called a bag men."

She eyed me with dull suspicion. "So, what do you want to know?"

"Well, for one thing, what does 'visiting the rat's mouth' mean?"

She frowned. "What are you talking about?"

"Last week, when Freddy Sanderling got poisoned, Aunt Edna said, 'It can't be Humpty because he was visiting the rat's mouth.'"

Sophia's frown deepened. "You know the expression, 'Let sleeping dogs lie?'"

I nodded. "Yes, ma'am."

"Then, I suggest you *do* that, Doreen. And while you're at it, clean the windows."

"But—"

Wheel of Fortune came back on. Sophia turned to face the TV and muttered, "Shut it."

Awesome. I guess the only window of opportunity for me involves Windex.

Chapter Fourteen

"Minestrone and bread sticks!" I said, taking my place at the lunch spread waiting for us at the picnic table in the courtyard. "Yum! I'm starved!"

"Glad you brought your appetite," Aunt Edna said. She smiled proudly and ladled me another spoonful of soup. "So, Sophia, you've been working our Dorey hard?"

"I tried," the old woman said. "But the sloth is strong in this one."

"What?" I grumbled. "I've been working my butt off!"

Jackie laughed and winked at me. "Looks like you've still got some of it left."

"Ha ha." I shoveled a spoonful of soup into my mouth. "Mmmmm. This is delicious!"

"Thanks." Aunt Edna took a seat beside me. "I'm glad *somebody* appreciates my cooking."

"I do, for sure," I said. "Hey, if you could have your famous grandmother cook something for you, what would it be?"

Aunt Edna laughed. "My ex-husband."

"Here here," Kitty said, raising her tea glass.

"Men," Sophia muttered. "Even when they're dead, their bodies are hard to get rid of."

"Here here," Kitty said again.

"So, what's on the afternoon agenda for our Dorey?" Aunt Edna asked.

I frowned. "I've already cleaned the kitchen, taken out the garbage, and wiped down the windows. What's left?"

"Have you changed her bedclothes yet?" Aunt Edna asked.

My nose crinkled. "No."

"Well, do that right after lunch and bring them to me. I need to get the laundry going. Oh, just the sheets, by the way. Not the plastic liners."

"Liners?" I asked. "Does Sophia wet the bed?"

"No," Sophia hissed. "They're on there in case there's a flood."

"Yeah," Jackie quipped. "By the Yellow River."

• • • •

"SO, YOU AND BRADY GETTING together again soon?" Kitty asked as we washed up the lunch dishes together.

"I don't know. We kind of had a spat."

"A spat?"

I gritted my teeth. "Maybe a little more than that. Geez, Kitty. It was mostly my fault. I lost my temper and said a few things."

"Like what?"

"I don't exactly remember. I'd had a bottle of red wine."

"Oh." Kitty put down her dishtowel and took my hand. "Well, all I can say is, when it comes to matters of the heart, it's best not to let sleeping dogs lie."

I frowned. "Sophia used that same expression on me this morning, only the opposite. That I should let them lie."

Kitty studied my face. "She did? About what?"

"About visiting the rat's mouth."

"What?"

"I asked her what the term means in mob lingo."

"Oh."

"Do you know?"

Kitty shook her head. "Nope. That's a new one on me."

I studied her face. "It is? Or do you just not want to tell me?"

Kitty laughed and put a hand on my shoulder. "You're still a newbie, Dorey. You can't expect Sophia—or any of us—to spill the beans about the Family to you all at once."

I frowned. "I guess."

"So, back to Brady. Don't let it fester between you two too long. Remember, boils have to be lanced for the healing to begin."

I grimaced. "Geez. Not a very romantic analogy."

Kitty shrugged. "Maybe not. But it's accurate just the same. Do you have your phone on you?"

"Yeah."

"Good. Call him. Do it now. I'll finish up here."

"Thanks. You're right." I pulled my cell phone from my pocket and went into my bedroom to make the call. But, like a chicken, at the last minute I freaked out and sent Brady a text instead.

I'm so sorry about last night. I just wanted you to take me seriously.

A few minutes later, after I'd chewed my thumbnail to the quick, Brady texted me back.

Believe me, I take what you did very seriously. I just didn't think you could be so spiteful. Better we just stay out of each other's way from now on.

My heart sunk. "Aww, crap!"

I fell back onto the bed. The phone rang in my hand.

"Brady?" I gasped into the speaker.

"No, it me, Kerri."

"Oh. Hi." I sat up on the bed. "What's up?"

"I just wanted to remind you about the celebration event at Eddie's car lot tomorrow. He's expecting the ads to bring a rush of customers, and wants you, his star, to be there to greet them. Are you still available to stay a few hours?"

I blew out a breath. "Sure."

Right now, I'm the most available person on the planet.

Chapter Fifteen

With all hopes of a love life spiraling down the drain, it was only fitting the Universe would have me spend the rest of the afternoon cleaning Sophia's bathroom.

After all, we were both washed up.

I'd no sooner scrubbed the tub clean when Sophia came in and announced she wanted to take a bath.

"Be careful," I warned. "It's so squeaky clean you might slip. I wouldn't want you to fall in and drown."

"Not a chance. I always keep one of these handy." She patted a package of adult diapers.

"What?" I asked, then immediately regretted it.

"These things can be used as flotation devices," she said.

I almost asked her how she knew that, but decided I desperately didn't want to know.

"Well, I'll leave you to it." I made a hasty exit, closing the door behind me. I was pretty sure that Sophia was crazy. But the old Queenpin was right about one thing—getting older sucked.

While Sophia puttered in the bathroom, I finished up the last of my chores by putting clean sheets on her bed. Stripped bare, I noticed her bed had two mattresses stacked atop each other. I laughed to myself. Sophia was as prickly as a cactus while she was conscious. Apparently she was just as touchy while she slept.

The Mafia madam was part *Princess and the Pea*. Or was it Princess and the *Pee*?

After amusing myself with that little gem, I got back to work. Given the amount of dust I'd found under Sophia's bed, I decided to give the mattresses a good whacking with the broom. After that, I vacuumed them, along with the rug. Finally, I put on the clean sheets, straightened the bedspread, and plumped the cushions.

I stood back and admired my work.

After this, there's no way Sophia can call me a sloth again.

With my list of chores dutifully completed, I went back and listened at the bathroom door. The water was still running.

"Everything okay in there?" I asked through the door.

"Fine. Now just let an old woman soak, would you?"

"You got it." I smiled, rubbed my hands together, and made my own clean getaway.

I had my own chores to do—including laundry. But when I got back to my room, the heap of dirty clothes were gone. I spied them hanging in the closet. Even my wine-stained white shirt, which I'd given up for dead, had been cleaned, pressed, and hung neatly away.

Gee. A girl could get used to this ...

• • • •

FOR ONCE, I WAS GRATEFUL that Aunt Edna served dinner promptly at four o'clock every afternoon. After getting Sophia fed and settled back into her cottage, I was off the hook for the rest of the evening.

Hmm...maybe that was her strategy all along.

I joined the other three ladies in the dining room. They were enjoying their evening ritual—playing cards and gossiping around the dining table.

"Pull up a chair," Kitty said, dealing me in. "You're one of us now."

"Thanks," I said. "And whoever did my laundry? I appreciate it."

"That was me." Aunt Edna elbowed. "Comes with the rent."

I grinned. "How'd you get all those stains out of my shirt?"

She shot me a look. "You really have to ask?"

"So when are you and Brady going out again?" Jackie asked.

I looked at my cards and sighed. "Never."

Jackie's eyes grew wide. "What happened?"

"I screwed things up. I thought it was a date. But it turns out, Brady just wanted to discuss Sophia's case."

"Oh." Aunt Edna laid her cards down on the table.

I cringed. "I got angry about it. Then I got a little drunk. I think I might've kicked his truck."

"His shiny F-150?" Aunt Edna asked.

"In my defense, he compared me to a prize fighter and a baseball double-hitter."

Aunt Edna shook her head. "Men. The only game they got nowadays is on ESPN."

"What did Brady want to know about Sophia?" Kitty asked.

I shook my head. "Nothing. He asked me if I thought anyone else could be involved in the plot to poison her. I said Humpty Bogart, then before I could explain that was a nickname, Brady laughed at me."

"Grrr," Kitty grumbled. "Nothing I hate more than when a man laughs at me!"

I smirked sourly. "What about when he grabs your ass?"

Aunt Edna's mouth fell open. "Brady grabbed your ass?"

"No." I scowled. "That dirtbag Eddie Houser did. The guy I shot the commercial for."

"Geez, Dorey," Kitty said. "Things don't work out for you and guys. First Tad. Now Brady. Eddie better watch his step."

"You aren't kidding." I grumbled.

Jackie closed her fan of cards. "Guys. Who needs 'em?"

"You've got a point there," Kitty said. "Why involve Brady? We can work on this case ourselves."

"Yeah," Aunt Edna said. "So, Dorey, why do you think Humpty's caught up in all this?"

I chewed my lip. "Because the guy Sophia saw delivering the cookies has a cleft chin. And Humpty has a cleft chin. But then, you said he couldn't have made the delivery because he was visiting the rat's mouth."

Kitty and I locked eyes. "What's that mean, Edna?" Kitty asked.

"What does *what* mean?"

"Visiting the rat's mouth," I said. "Is that mob speak for something?"

Aunt Edna frowned. "No. That's just what I call Boca Raton. I only meant Humpty couldn't have done the drop because he was out of town in Boca, that's all."

"Oh." I slumped in my chair.

"Wait a minute," Kitty said. "That Melanie character told me she had a greenhouse in Boca Raton. I bet that's where she grew the poisonous manchineel fruits."

"I guess the cops will find out when they search the place," Jackie said.

"Maybe they will, maybe they won't," I said. "We caught Melanie red-handed with the poisonous fruit. What need do the police have to search the greenhouse for more?"

Kitty pursed her lips. "Hmm. Maybe the cops don't need to, but whoever was working with her just might—if they plan on destroying the evidence, that is."

"Or gather up more fruits and try to finish the job," Aunt Edna said.

We all exchanged glances.

Aunt Edna frowned. "So when Humpty went to Boca, you think he could've been going to visit Melanie at her greenhouse?"

"It's possible," I said. "Sophia told me she thought Melanie was too dumb to come up with the scheme all on her own. I agree."

"Kinda sketchy if you ask me," Jackie said. "Lots of people go to Boca. And lots of people have cleft chins."

"True enough," Aunt Edna said. "But what's the harm in asking Humpty for a little more information?"

"We might spook him," I said. "We could put a tail out on him and see what he's up to."

"In the Kia?" Aunt Edna said. "That thing sticks out like one of Jackie's outfits."

"Ask Morty to do it," Kitty said.

Aunt Edna scowled. "We don't need guys messing this up. We can handle this ourselves."

"Why not?" I said. "After all, this *is* Family business."

Kitty smiled and laid down her hand. "All for one, and one for all!"

"Like the four Mouseketeers!" Jackie said.

"Musketeers," Aunt Edna said.

"What?" Jackie cocked her head. "So, you saying I shouldn't order us some Minnie Mouse hats?"

Aunt Edna rolled her yes. "Yes. That's exactly what I'm saying."

"Ooh," Kitty cooed, rubbing her hands together. "The only thing I like more than proving a man wrong is proving him guilty."

"I dunno," I said. "I like proving them wrong more."

Kitty laughed. "Who am I kidding? So do I."

Aunt Edna smiled coyly. "Jackie, put a pot of coffee on. We got some man-splaining to do."

Chapter Sixteen

In the moonlight, I could make out the shadowy figure of someone in the hoodie walking toward me. My heart involuntarily skipped a beat. I was standing in the dark in front of Sophia's cottage at 5:29 in the morning. I had to give it to them—the ScarBux delivery person was right on time.

"I'll take that," I said as he drew closer.

"Who are *you*?" a man's voice asked.

"I'm helping out the elderly woman who lives here."

"Sophia?"

My shoulders stiffened. "You know her name?"

"Sure!" the youthful sounding voice under the hoodie said. "I hope she's okay. She's such a sweetheart."

My nose crinkled. "Are you sure you've got the right address?"

He laughed and handed me a paper sack. "That'll be ten bucks even."

"Ten bucks for a cup of coffee?"

"For *two* cups."

"Oh." I gave the guy a twenty. He handed me back a five and five ones. I smirked and gave him back two bucks.

He grinned. "Thanks. Same time tomorrow?"

"Sure."

He turned to go. "Tell Sophia I said hi."

"Okay. What's your name?"

"Chase."

"Right. Will do, Chase."

As Chase turned and sprinted back to his car, I noted that he looked like your ordinary, average, athletic young man. He was probably in his early twenties. And one more thing—Chase was utterly devoid of a cleft in his chin.

My mind flashed back to the stranger standing in the street at Sundial—the one who'd jabbed at me menacingly after my disastrous non-date with Brady. He or she was probably just some drunk loser, or some young punk checking for unlocked doors in hopes of scoring some spare change.

I shrugged it off. Whoever they'd been they probably hadn't even been looking at me. I shook my head softly.

What is it with all these hoodies nowadays, anyway?

The aroma of fresh coffee snagged my wandering attention. I peeked inside the ScarBux sack. Sophia had called in a double order. I smiled. Maybe she didn't think I was such a sloth after all.

I pulled out one of the cups, punched in the lid's sipper hole, and took a taste. The coffee was so strong and bitter it made my face pucker.

Yuck. Now I know how Sophia powers up that bad attitude of hers ...

I climbed the three steps leading up to the front porch of the Queenpin's cottage and slipped the key into the lock. Slowly, I opened the door and tiptoed into her apartment, trying not to make a sound. The way I saw it, the longer the old lady slept, the shorter my day with her would be.

I set the sack with the other coffee on the kitchen counter. Suddenly, the ceiling lamp flicked on like a floodlight, blinding me where I stood.

"It's about time," a cranky voice grumbled.

Squinting in the harsh light, I made out the visage of Doña Sophia hobbling into the kitchen in her bathrobe. It was the first time I'd seen her without her silver turban. No wonder she wore it. Her hair was as thin on top as a desperate man's comb-over.

"Why are you drinking my coffee?" she growled.

"What?" I fumbled. "No. I ... uh ..."

"Both of those are for *me!*" Sophia snatched the cup from my hand. "A sloth *and* a thief," she muttered. "What am I going to do with you?"

Fire me?

Please?

• • • •

AFTER POURING SOPHIA'S bootleg ScarBux into a real cup and saucer, I settled her on the couch. Then I made her bed to the sounds of *Wheel of Fortune* blasting on the TV. Mercifully, my first order from the old lady was to check on breakfast. I was happy for the break.

I marched over to Aunt Edna's to find her sitting at the dining room table looking haggard as she sipped her own mug of coffee.

"Morning," I said. "You look tired."

She waved my comment away like it was a pesky fly. "I was up a little last night. I couldn't stop thinking about what you said. You really think Humpty could be trying to poison Sophia?"

I shrugged. "I don't know. It's just a theory. But one thing I know for sure, Sophia's ready for her breakfast now. For an old lady, she's sure got a heck of an appetite."

"Don't I know it. Hey, wait a minute. I know. Why don't I make her breakfast in bed? That way we can discuss this Humpty matter with Kitty and Jackie without Sophia horning in."

"Sounds good to me."

"Me, too," Jackie said, appearing from around a corner.

Aunt Edna hauled herself up from the table. "If Melanie really *was* working with Humpty or somebody else, we need to keep a sharp eye on anything Sophia eats. They could still be trying to poison her."

"What's to worry about?" Jackie asked, following her into the kitchen. "Since Sophia ain't in the nursing home no more, we control every morsel she eats, and every sip she takes."

I grimaced. "Uh ... except for one."

Aunt Edna's eyes narrowed in on me. "What are you talking about, Dorey?"

I cringed. I hated to be a snitch, but this was important. Besides, Sophia already thought I was a sloth and a thief. What did it matter if she added rat to my list of attributes?

"Coffee," I said. "Sophia gets coffee delivered every morning."

"What?" Aunt Edna dropped the spoon in her hand. It clattered to the kitchen floor.

I bent down to pick it up. "Uh ... sorry. Sophia gets her morning coffee delivered from ScarBux." I flinched as I added, "She thinks it's better than yours."

"Excuse me?" Aunt Edna growled, her face lighting up like a red balloon. She picked up her rolling pin.

I showed her my empty palms. "Hey, I don't agree with her. I tried the stuff this morning. That ScarBux crap is as bitter as p ..."

My face dropped an inch. "Poison."

The three of us exchanged glances.

Aunt Edna shook her head. "If that doesn't ... How long have you known?"

"Only about a week," I said. "Sophia swore me to silence about it."

"An Omertà?" Aunt Edna whacked her palm with the rolling pin. "She made you take an oath of silence about her stupid ..." She gritted her teeth and glared at me like a bulldog. "I should whack—"

"I'm sorry!" I blurted. "At the time, I didn't think it was important. But I do, now. Please. Don't hit me with that!"

"Huh?" Aunt Edna glanced down at her hands and seemed to suddenly realize she was brandishing her rolling pin like a lethal weapon. She tucked it in her apron and hugged me. "Dorey, I'd never whack you with my rolling pin. Now Sophia, on the other hand—"

"Uh, shouldn't we be getting that coffee away from Sophia?" Jackie asked.

Aunt Edna let go of her bear hug on me and began barking orders. "Dorey! Get back over there right now and get that crappy coffee away from Sophia. Then take it over to Kitty to test. Go! Now!"

"But how?" I asked. "Sophia nearly bit my head off when she found out I took a sip."

"That's *your* problem," Aunt Edna said. "I've got breakfast to make."

Jackie put a hand on my shoulder. "We can double-team her, Dorey. Do a little switcheroo."

"What do you mean?"

Jackie winked. "Just follow my lead."

"Hard not to, considering you look like a traffic light in that red shirt and green pants," I quipped.

"Hey, in my day, I could stop traffic another way, if you catch my drift."

"Would you two get out of here, already?" Aunt Edna grumbled.

Jackie grabbed the half-full coffee carafe from the kitchen counter and headed for the front door. As I followed behind her, I saw Aunt Edna open the fridge and rub her hands together. Her expression was pure evil genius.

"So the Queenpin don't like my coffee, eh?" I heard my aunt mutter to herself. "Well, this morning she's getting a special breakfast in bed. And I know just what to make. Eggs Benedict-Arnold."

Chapter Seventeen

Jackie's coffee switcheroo had worked. While Sophia watched the news with a cupful of Aunt Edna's coffee, my aunt got busy preparing the Queenpin's "special breakfast."

What made it special, I didn't want to know...

Meanwhile, Jackie was standing watch like a red-and-green beacon outside Kitty's front door, while Kitty and I got busy testing the Scar-Bux coffee in the secret laboratory Kitty had in her spare bedroom. If Dr. Frankenstein had been a woman, she'd have been Kitty Corleone.

"Hmm, none of the usual suspects," Kitty said, peering through pink lab goggles at the clear, plastic thingy she was holding up to the light. Inside the plastic cube, different colored stripes ran up and down like a bar chart.

"What do you mean?" I asked.

Kitty frowned. "If this coffee was poisoned, it wasn't cyanide, arsenic, or even manchineel."

I chewed my bottom lip. "Hopefully, for Sophia's sake, it wasn't poisoned at all."

Kitty pursed her lips. "It's looking that way. But I've got to run some more tests before I can call it safe." She set the plastic testing kit on the concrete lab counter and turned to me. "Dorey, you've been working with Sophia for the past couple of days. Has she mentioned any complaints?"

My right eyebrow rose an inch. "Are you kidding me?"

Kitty laughed and rolled her eyes. "I mean beyond her usual grumblings. You know, weird stuff."

I crossed my arms. "She said I was a sloth and a thief. Does that count?"

"Naw. She calls everybody that. I mean, did she say anything about *herself*. You know, body aches, constipation, diarrhea, gas, that kind of thing?"

I grimaced. "No."

Thank goodness.

"Huh," Kitty grunted.

"Oh, wait. I remember Sophia saying the other day that her hair had gone silver and her butt had turned to lead."

Kitty laughed. "Sounds like Sophia, all right. Did you notice any stains or powder residue on her clothes or bedsheets when you changed them?"

"Uh ... no. But I wasn't exactly looking for any."

"Right." Kitty reached for a blue bottle on one of the lab shelves. "Why would you, when she's always wearing that ratty old shawl of hers, right? It's like her security blanket or something."

"Huh. That reminds me. Yesterday morning after breakfast, Sophia was hanging up her shawl and complained that her shoulders were always cold and her feet were hot."

Kitty rubbed her lips with her index finger. "Hmm. That could just be poor circulation. At any rate, until further notice, no more ScarBux for the Queenpin."

I blew out a breath. "Great. I can't wait to break the news to her. She'll probably put a hit out on me."

Kitty shot me a smirk. "Hey. Good thing you only took a tiny sip of that coffee. If it had been laced with cyanide, you'd already be dead."

• • • •

AFTER SERVING SOPHIA her "special breakfast" and fluffing up the couch cushions, I went back to Aunt Edna's and joined the three mob molls sitting around the breakfast table.

"I still have a few tests to run, but as far as I can tell, the coffee isn't being poisoned," Kitty said.

"Not even with them fruits?" Jackie asked.

Kitty shook her head. "Not even with beach apples."

"Why would anyone want to poison Sophia now anyway?" Jackie asked, setting down her coffee cup. "She ain't got no money."

"Maybe not," Aunt Edna said. "But she's still got the power. Sophia still ain't named her heir. So that means the position for new head of the Family is still up for grabs."

My mind flashed to a horde of gangsters in pinstripe suits with Tommy guns lining up to become the next leader of a bunch of old ladies who were in bed by 9:30. I snickered.

"What's so funny?" Aunt Edna asked.

I straightened up in my chair and scrambled for something to say. "Nothing. I ... uh ... I just wish I could prove to Sophia that she's wrong about me. I'm not a sloth or a thief. Can you believe she called me lazy, even after I hit the mattresses for her, for crying out loud?"

Aunt Edna stared at me. "Sophia told you to hit the mattresses?"

I shook my head. "No. I took the initiative. See? I'm no sloth. I did it while she was in the shower."

"You and who else?" Kitty asked.

I shrugged. "Nobody. What? You all don't think I can hit a couple of mattresses all by myself? Geez! What kind of wimp do you people think I am?"

"That ain't what we're saying, right ladies?" Aunt Edna said.

Kitty and Jackie nodded. "Right."

I glanced at the gaudy gold cherub staring down at us from the clock on the wall. It was half past nine. "Oh, crap. I've got to get ready and go."

"Where to?" Jackie asked.

I sprang up from my chair. "I've got an appointment with Crazy Eddie." I shook my head. "Believe me, it's the last thing I want to do, but a contract's a contract. I can't get out of it."

"Uh-huh," Aunt Edna said. "Crazy Eddie, eh?"

"Yeah." I laid my breakfast dishes in the sink. "It'll all be over with today. Then, with any luck, things will get back to normal."

"Right," Aunt Edna said.

I turned back around from the sink to see the three women staring at me. "Oh! Hey, can one of you take care of Sophia this morning?"

"Take care of her?" Kitty asked.

"Yeah. Go get the breakfast dishes? And tell Sophia I'll be back before she even notices I'm gone. Hopefully, she won't mind. Tell her I'm doing this for the Family. We could use the money, right?"

"Sure," Aunt Edna said.

"I'll watch Sophia until you get back," Jackie said.

I smiled. "Thanks, Jackie."

Jackie nodded. "Sure thing. You can count on me."

I grinned like the Cheshire cat. "I'll show Sophia I'm not lazy. I'm ... *scrappy*."

"You ain't scrappy, kid," Aunt Edna said.

I frowned. "I'm not?"

My aunt shook her head. "No. Scrappy means you settle for scraps. From what I see, you're after the whole enchilada."

I grinned. "Thanks. I'm trying."

Chapter Eighteen

Just when I thought I'd survived my showdown with the tourniquet jeans of death, they'd gone and made a second attempt on my life.

"Kerri, you owe me *big time* for this," I grumbled through the bathroom door at Crazy Eddie's Used Cars.

"For the jeans, or the bathroom?" she asked.

"Both," I hissed.

I leaned against the sticky, mustard-colored wall to brace myself, then sucked in my stomach and forced the button on the waistband closed. Cinched nearly in half, I peered in the cracked mirror at my teased hair and makeup.

Ugh! I don't know what I did in a past life to deserve this, but I sure hope I don't do it again.

No longer able to breathe for more reasons than one, I burst through the bathroom door in full Daisy-the-Price-Slayer regalia. I waved a hand in front of my face. "Whew! That place ought to be labeled a biological hazard zone."

Kerri cringed. "Sorry. After this, you're off the hook, I promise." She grabbed my elbow to support me as I wobbled like a newborn colt in the six-inch stilettos.

"I'd better be." I stared past a couple of cheap office desks through a wall of plate glass windows. Outside in the car lot, a gigantic inflatable gorilla stared back at me. Balloons and banners festooned every junker car I could see.

"Eddie sure pulled out all the cliché stops for this one, didn't he?" I quipped.

Kerri whispered in my ear, "You haven't even seen the clowns or the corndog cart yet."

My upper lip snarled. "Speaking of corndogs, I'd like to stick one right up Eddie's—"

"I get the picture," Kerri said. "You ready?"

"Lead the way. The sooner we get started, the sooner this car crash will be over."

Kerri stopped in front of the exit door and turned to face me. "Have you seen the commercial yet?"

"No." I swatted a lock of afro hair away from my face. "And I hope I never do."

"I've got it right here on my phone. Maybe it'll get you more ... *in the spirit*."

"Fine."

Kerri clicked her phone and handed it to me. As I watched the video play on the display, whatever dignity I had left shriveled up and blew away like a dung ball in the Sahara.

"So, you feel in character now?" Kerri asked.

"Sure."

If that character's Arnold Schwarzenegger and we're about to film The Terminator ...

• • • •

I BATTED AN ERRANT balloon away from my face and followed Kerri into the fray of used cars, carny workers, and chaos. She stopped short in front of a small crowd of people.

"What a sad-sack circus this is," I grumbled, nearly running into the back of her. "This dump is the last place I want to be."

"Uh ... Doreen," Kerri said. "I want you to meet Eddie's wife, Kareena."

I laughed, "As in *careening* out of control?"

"It's Kareena with a *K*," a woman's gravelly voice said.

I gulped. So much for making a good impression. But then again, Kareena wasn't that impressive, either. The middle-aged woman was too tan, too red-headed, and too old for her outfit. A moment earlier, she'd been puffing Virginia Slims and talking to someone with a microphone. But now her beady eyes were locked on me.

"I take it you're that psycho killer chick Eddie hired," she said, a sneer creasing her hard face. She lit another cigarette off the burning end of her last one. "You don't want to be here? Too bad. We paid you. You're ours for the next two hours."

"So nice to see you again," Kerri said, stepping between us. "Everything looks so ... festive! Where's Eddie?"

Kareena's face shifted from haughty to annoyed. "I dunno. He ain't showed up yet." She shot me a nasty look. "Hey, bimbo chick. You two got something going on I don't know about?"

"No, ma'am!" I blurted.

"Ma'am!" Kareena screeched. "Who you callin' ma'am?"

"Take it easy," a young man standing beside her said. He put a hand on Kareena's shoulder. "I'm sure she only meant it as a sign of respect."

I nodded too rapidly. "Yes, he's right. I only meant it like that. I swear."

"Hi, I'm Racer," the guy said. "Eddie's son."

"Something ain't right," Kareena said. "Eddie wouldn't miss this shindig for the world." She laughed bitterly. "Mr. Top Dog's always got to mark his territory." She eyed me with suspicion and disgust. "When's the last time you saw him?"

"Wednesday, when we shot the commercial," I said.

Kareena's laser glare shifted to Kerri. "And you?"

"Same for me," Kerri said. "But I talked to him briefly yesterday, and sent him a copy of the commercial for his approval."

"That so, eh?" Kareena said. She put her hands on her hips, causing a cascade of twinkling gold bangles to collide at her wrists.

I studied Kareena's jaded face. Suddenly, I realized she had a cleft chin. So did her son, Racer!

I took a step away from Kerri and was about to go call Aunt Edna with the news when I noticed that the guy selling corndogs also had a cleft chin. So did the clown handing out balloons.

Ugh! What's with all the cleft chins nowadays?

I turned back around and nearly groaned. Some guy in the bad suit was walking up to us. He also had—you guessed it—a cleft chin.

So much for that *clue.*

"Hey, where's Eddie already?" he asked.

"If I knew, Brad, don't you think I'd have dragged him here by now?" Kareena said.

"Uh, who's gonna run the raffle to win the hundred dollar gift certificate for Scooters Wings & Dings?" Brad asked.

Kareena rolled her eyes. "Seeing as you're our top salesman, I'm putting you in charge."

"What does Eddie say?" Brad asked.

"Eddie ain't here, you dimwit!" Kareena screeched.

"Um ... excuse me," I said. "Brad, when did you see Eddie last?"

"Yesterday afternoon." Brad pulled at his collar with his index finger. "We got a trade-in. A lime-green Nissan Cube. Eddie took it out for a test drive."

"When did he come back?" I asked.

"I don't know. I took off early yesterday." Brad cupped his hand like a visor over his eyes and scanned the parking lot. "I don't see the Cube. Maybe he took it home last night."

"Taking a strange one home," Kareena grumbled. "Sounds like Eddie, all right."

I turned to Kareena. "When did Eddie get home last night?"

She glared at me from beneath her cherry-red bangs. "How should I know? We ain't lived together for over six months now."

"Oh, I'm sorry," I said, dancing inside with joy. "I guess that means this whole 'shindig' is cancelled, then. What a shame."

Kareena snorted. "Not on your life, toots. Me and Eddie had our differences, sure. But we had *one* thing in common. We always demanded our money's worth."

Chapter Nineteen

A torrent of sweat streamed down my back. At the moment, it was taking all the acting talent I could muster not to stab someone to death.

Kerri had abandoned me for another appointment just as people were arriving at Crazy Eddie's Used Cars in droves. The problem was, most of them weren't customers. They were women—angry women with picket signs. Signs with Eddie Houser's name on them and a pig face crossed out inside a red circle.

While I totally concurred with the sentiment, it couldn't be good for business. Five percent of nothing was ... *nothing*.

"How can you humiliate yourself like that?" one of the woman shouted at me as I stood next to a rusted out Chevy Malibu, pointing my rubber sword at its "Crazy-Eddie-Low" price sticker.

My face grew hot. My arm went limp. "Uh ... it's just a job."

I looked away from the woman and made a half-hearted attempt to slash the price on the windshield. I knew right then I'd sunk the absolute lowest a human could go without becoming a politician.

"Come on, you can do better than that," a voice rang out.

I recognized it immediately. It belonged to Shirley Saurwein.

Seriously, Universe?

I ground my molars and looked up at the sky.

Come on, stupid meteor!

"If you're looking for salvation for your dignity, that ship has sailed," Saurwein said.

I glared at her and hissed, "What are *you* doing here?"

Saurwein grinned and cracked her gum between her bright-red lips. "You kiddin'? I wouldn't miss this encore performance for the world. Where's Eddie? I could use some juicy soundbites from that idiot."

I scowled. "Eddie's a no-show."

Saurwein's blonde eyebrow ticked up a notch. "You don't say."

"He probably skipped town," I quipped. "After meeting his wife, I could hardly blame him."

"Hey!" a woman shouted from the growing mob of picketers. "Aren't you that reporter from the *Beach Gazette*?"

Saurwein stuck her chin out and smiled. "Yours truly."

"I thought so," the woman growled. "Your portrayal of women in that rag is almost as bad as Eddie's in that commercial!"

"Yeah," another woman yelled. "Those two poor little old ladies you smeared in the last issue. What's wrong with loving an iguana, anyway?"

"Last I heard, there's laws against bestiality," Saurwein yelled back, then laughed.

Someone in the crowd hollered a string of obscenities, punctuated by hurtling a half-eaten corndog right at Saurwein. I smirked as the greasy projectile hit the brassy reporter right above the crotch of her white pants.

"Very funny," Saurwein hissed. She grabbed a tissue from her pocket and swiped at the mustard stain commemorating the corndog's inaugural landing. "Anybody throw anything else at me and I'll have the lot of you arrested for assault!"

The women glared at us. We glared back. The parking lot standoff lasted about a minute, until the corndog hurler said, "Come on, ladies. Let's not waste any more time with these pathetic examples of womankind. Let's take our protest to the streets."

After quite a few choice facial and finger expressions aimed our way, the gang of picketers turned and headed toward the sidewalk running along US 19.

I shook my head at Saurwein. "I can't believe I'm saying this, but I think I owe you one."

"More than one," Saurwein said. "I counted fourteen of those broads."

I fidgeted with the rubber chicken filet squashing my left boob. "Hey. Do you know what time is it?"

"Five minutes to two. Why? You got a hot date with Jethro Bodine?"

"Ha ha." I scowled. "No. In five minutes, my time is up."

Saurwein smirked. "I think your time's been up for a few years now, honey."

I gritted my teeth. "That's not what I—"

"I know. But geez, Diller. You make it so easy."

• • • •

"WHERE DO YOU THINK you're going?" Kareena asked as I slammed the driver's door on The Toad.

"You got your two hours' worth," I said. "I'm getting out of here before those women over there start throwing Molotov cocktails." I turned the key in the ignition. Nothing but click.

Crap! Why now?

I popped the hood latch, grabbed the socket wrench, and kicked open the door.

"Hey, what are you doing?" Kareena growled as I climbed out. I turned to see she'd pulled a small pistol from her bra and had it pointed right at me.

"What?" I squealed. "I ... I was just going to bang on the solenoid."

"Like you 'banged' Eddie?"

My face twisted with disgust. "No offense, but Eddie Houser is the last person on Earth I'd want to bang."

Kareena glared at me. "You think you're better than us? That me and Eddie are just two-bit used-car hustlers? Well, let me tell you something, missy. Every single car in this lot is better than that hunk of junk you're driving."

I hoped Kareena's aim with a gun wasn't as good as it was with an insult. I gathered up the last of my gumption and said, "You know, Kareena. You're absolutely right. Sorry for the confusion. Just let me get this hunk of junk started, and I'll be on my way."

"Humph. You should trade that thing in. I've got a nice Plymouth Breeze in the back lot that—"

"Thanks," I said, whacking the Kia's solenoid. "Maybe another time. One when you're not holding me at gunpoint."

"Oh. Sure."

Kareena tucked the pistol back into her left bra cup, then began to pull something out of the right one. I held my breath, wondering if she was going to pull out a switchblade and finish me off. She took a step toward me.

"What are you doing?" I asked, tightening the grip on the socket wrench.

"Here," she said, whipping out a business card. "Take my card. I'll make you the best price in town."

Numb with shock, I took the card.

Kareena grinned and slapped me on the back. "You can't do better than Crazy Eddie's. I guarantee it."

I shook my head.

Unbelievable. This woman's got more balls than Willy Loman.

As Kareena turned and walked away, a thought made me swallow a knot in my throat.

Geez. I hope this isn't a remake of Death of a Salesman.

Chapter Twenty

I was halfway home when I realized I was being tailed.

Ever since I'd left Crazy Eddie's and turned off US 19 onto 22nd Avenue North, a blue Ford Taurus with tinted windows had been ducking around traffic, keeping a low profile as it stayed about a football field length behind me.

My mind went haywire with paranoia.

Who could be after me? Kareena? One of those ladies at the protest? Humpty Bogart? Sammy the Psycho? The cleft-chin guy from Sundial? Brady?

I glanced in the rearview mirror again and chewed my bottom lip. What was wrong with my life that I could easily name half a dozen people who might want to knock my lights out?

I sped through the yellow light at the intersection of 22nd Avenue and 16th Street. Two blocks down, I took a right on a side street, then worked my way back to Palm Court Cottages, zigzagging every couple of streets just to be sure I wasn't being followed.

Keeping an eye out for the blue Taurus, I circled the block before finally pulling in and parking in front of Aunt Edna's place. As I climbed out of the Kia, a car caught my eye. But it wasn't the blue Taurus. It was a lime-green Nissan Cube parked two spaces down.

What the?

Still dressed like Daisy the Price Slasher, I kicked off the stilettos and hobbled barefoot over to the ugly, neon-green box of a car. The windows were tinted dark, making it hard to see inside.

I tried the door handle. It opened. The car was empty—except for the blood splatter covering pretty much the entire front seat compartment.

"Hell!" I screeched, then lost my balance and nearly fell head first into the grisly scene. My right hand caught the driver's headrest. I grabbed it and pushed off, propelling my torso out of the car. I stared at the scene for another second, then quickly slammed the door.

Panic shot down my spine. Was that *Eddie's* blood? What the hell was his car doing in front of my place?

The rattle of an engine made me look up. Half a block away, a blue Taurus was heading my way. I couldn't make out the driver through the darkened windshield. Scared witless, I stood, paralyzed, as the car drew nearer, then stopped right in front of me.

The driver's side window went down a few inches. I saw the glint of something metal. Then a flash.

"Don't shoot!" I screamed.

Chapter Twenty-One

"What the hell's going on, Diller?" Saurwein called out from the blue Taurus. She rolled the driver's side window down a couple more inches, aimed her camera, and took another shot of me.

"Argh!" I growled, anger eclipsing my panic. "Why are you following me?"

Saurwein shrugged. "Because you always make such an interesting subject. That, and my in-laws are staying with us. Believe me, I'm in no hurry to get home."

"Well, I don't care—"

"Hey, what's with the blood?" Saurwein asked.

"Blood?"

"Yeah, the red stuff all over your hands."

I looked at my bloody palms and nearly screamed again. I willed myself to keep calm.

"Oh ... I ... uh ... I fell down wearing those stupid stilettos. Scraped my palms up pretty bad."

"Uh-huh."

I scowled. "You know what, Saurwein? You following me home has got to be against the law. Stalking. Harassment. Something. Unless you leave me alone this instant, I'll figure out a way to charge you with something."

"Uh-huh," Saurwein grunted. She snapped another picture of me, then put her camera away and eyed me up and down. "You know what, Diller? You should get some sun."

"Sun?"

"Yeah. Because in my book, right now you're looking shadier than shit."

• • • •

I MADE SURE SAURWEIN was gone, then I scrambled into the azalea hedges lining Aunt Edna's house.

What in the world is Eddie's car doing here? Should I call the cops? Should I tell Aunt Edna?

I crawled on hands and knees behind the hedges and over to the garden spigot. I was barely able to keep it together until I could wash off whoever's horrible blood was on my hands.

I turned on the rusty tap and rubbed my palms together under the stream of lukewarm water. Mesmerized and horrified, I stared at the ground as the reddish water seeped into the soil below the spigot.

Suddenly, I felt a hand on my shoulder.

"What'cha doing, Dorey?" Jackie asked, kneeling beside me.

"Yaaugh!" I squealed. "How do you do that?"

"Do what?"

"Sneak up on people like that."

Jackie stood up and shrugged. "It's a gift."

I turned off the tap and hoisted myself to standing. "I'm uh ... just washing up. I—"

"Come inside," Jackie said calmly. Her boney fingers curled around the back of my neck. "We've been waiting for you."

Chapter Twenty-Two

I was sitting on my hands in Aunt Edna's "good chair." It was a brown, vinyl recliner that had probably made its advertising debut on *The Lawrence Welk Show*.

Across the room, perched on my aunt's olive-green couch, sat my aunt, Kitty, and Jackie. They stared at me like a trio of Judge Judies. I couldn't help but notice all the velveteen curtains had been drawn shut.

Under their narrow-eyed scrutiny, I began to fidget—and wonder if the ancient Barcalounger I was sitting in had come with an electrocution switch. I prayed the chair was too old to have come with a remote. A quick scan of the women's hands showed they were empty. But their faces were full of worry.

"Uh ... what's wrong?" I asked, forcing a twitchy smile.

"You seem to be taking matters into your own hands now, Dorey," Aunt Edna said. "Were you gonna fill us in on the plan?"

"The plan?" I asked. "What plan?"

Aunt Edna's face grew taut. "It ain't proper protocol, Dorey. Maybe you didn't know no better, being so new to the garbage business and all. But you should've gone through the proper channels before you went and hit the mattresses with Eddie Houser."

"What?" I balked. "I didn't sleep with Eddie Houser! Gross!"

"Who's talking about screwing the guy?" Jackie asked. "I'm confused here."

"You and me both," I said, turning back to my aunt. "Why are you saying I'm sleeping with Eddie Houser?"

"I ain't," Aunt Edna said. "I'm talking about *hitting the mattresses*, Dorey. You told us yourself. Don't deny it."

"Well, sure," I said, relieved they didn't think I'd killed the guy. "What's the big deal?"

Jackie's eyes grew wider. "What'd you use? A bat?"

"No. A broom."

Jackie cringed. "Ouch."

My brow furrowed. "What else was I supposed to use to beat the dust off Sophia's old mattresses?"

The women's faces went slack.

Kitty cleared her throat. "Doreen, "*hitting the mattresses* means starting a war with a rival clan."

I gulped. "It does? I didn't know that."

"What did you think it meant, then?" Kitty asked.

I scooted to the edge of the Barcalounger. "What I just said. You know, to beat the dust out of Sophia's mattresses."

Aunt Edna shook her head slowly. "And I suppose you also didn't know that Eddie Houser was a known associate of Humphrey Bogaratelli, either."

"What?" I felt the air drain from my lungs. "No. I didn't."

"Huh," Kitty said.

I grimaced. "Look. All I did was go see Eddie to—"

"We know all about it, Dorey," Aunt Edna said, cutting me off. "Amateur move, just leaving the body out there to be found."

"Body?" I gulped. "You mean ... in that Nissan? You saw his body?"

"Yeah," Jackie said. "And you didn't do the deed with no cuticle scissors this time, that's for sure."

My shoulders slumped. "But I ... I didn't ..."

"You don't gotta worry about it," Jackie said. "We took care of it."

My eyebrows jumped up an inch. "You three got rid of Eddie's body?"

"Not us," Aunt Edna said. "We called Victor to do it. We look out for our own around here." Aunt Edna's eyes narrowed in on mine. "So, you looking out for *us*, too?"

"I ... I ..."

Aunt Edna sighed. "Dorey, Dorey, Dorey. You vying to be the new Queenpin, or what?"

I nearly fell out of the Barcalounger. "What? No! Why would I? Listen. This is all a big misunderstanding."

Jackie laughed. "Well, that ain't no consolation to Eddie, now, is it?"

I shook my head in dismay. "Why would I kill Eddie? You just told me he's part of the Family!"

"You don't got to be outside the Family to be *outside the Family*, if you know what I mean," Aunt Edna said.

"A traitor's a traitor," Kitty said.

"Why'd you kill him?" Aunt Edna asked. "Is Eddie working with Humpty to poison Sophia? Or maybe they're in cahoots to steal from the Family Fund?"

"Humpty's been eatin' alone for a long time," Kitty said, rubbing her chin. "You thinking maybe Eddie was his secret lunch partner?"

I stared at the three ladies in disbelief. "I ... I don't know."

Aunt Edna chewed her bottom lip. "Either way, you could've just stirred up a hornet's nest, Dorey. We need to take this to the consigliere."

"The what?"

"The *consigliere*," Kitty said. "The Family adviser. He's supposed to be consulted before decisions that big are made."

"Oh." My mind flashed to some horrible old man in a wheelchair, ready to put his lit cigar out in my eyeball.

"Who's the consigliere?" I asked.

"Morty." Jackie said.

"But first, we've got a few loose ends to tie up," Kitty said.

"Uh ... loose ends?" I squeaked.

"Yeah," Jackie said. "We couldn't find the weapon. What'd you do with the broom?"

"I didn't kill Eddie with a broom!" I said.

"So you was lying?" Jackie asked. "Ah. You used the bat, didn't you?"

My jaw went slack. "The bat?"

"Yeah. The baseball bat I gave you," Jackie said. "Where is it?"

"Uh ... it's still in the Kia."

Aunt Edna shook her head and blew out a breath. "Another amateur move."

• • • •

"SO THIS IS WHAT YOU used to bust Eddie up with, eh?" Jackie said, pulling a bloody baseball bat from the trunk of The Toad.

I stared at the bat in horror. I'd been driving around all day with that thing in the trunk! "I ... I—"

"Louisville Slugger," Kitty said, examining it with a pink-handled magnifying lens. "A classic."

"Bag it," Aunt Edna said, glancing around. "We got to get rid of the evidence. Pronto."

"I'm on it," Jackie said.

Kitty held open a black garbage bag. Jackie dropped the bat inside.

"Now what?" Kitty asked, pulling the bag's string tight.

"We go see Morty," Aunt Edna said. "Jackie, you stay with Sophia. We don't need her knowing about this. Capeesh?"

Jackie nodded. "You got it, Capo."

"Good. Kitty, you come with us. Shove the bat under the driver's seat. Doreen, you drive."

"But I ..." I stuttered.

"No more excuses," my aunt said, dropping the keys into my palm. "You made this mess. You gotta do your part to clean it up."

Unable to figure out where to even begin to try and explain, I gave up and nodded. I climbed into the driver's seat and turned the key in The Toad's ignition.

Nothing but click. *Again.*

"Well, that makes two dead in one day," Kitty quipped.

"This ain't funny," Aunt Edna said, handing me the socket wrench. "You know the drill, Dorey. At least we know *that* for sure."

"Fine," I said. "I'll do it. I just wish you'd given me time to change. These jeans are killing me."

"Now you know how Eddie felt," Aunt Edna said.

What?

I climbed out of the Kia, unlatched the hood, and got busy beating the life out of the solenoid. I didn't need any motivation to perform the act.

Aunt Edna thinks I'm a murderer. That I'm trying to take over the Family! She hates me! How could this get any worse?

Then, as if a magic genie had granted my wish, I instantly saw how it could get worse.

A police cruiser was headed our way. And behind the wheel was Officer Gregory Brady himself.

Chapter Twenty-Three

"Car trouble, ladies?" Brady asked as he slowly steered his police cruiser up beside The Toad until his window was even with Aunt Edna's.

"We're fine," Aunt Edna said. "Dorey's taking care of it."

"Is that so." Brady inched the cruiser forward until he spotted me hiding behind the raised hood. His grin evaporated.

"Nothing happening here," I said, my voice at least an octave above normal. I forced a trembling smile. "I mean, nothing that we can't deal with on our own. You know, all by little old selves."

Little-old selves? Really, Doreen?

My heart thumped so loud I was sure he could hear it. I tried to whack the solenoid again, but my fumbling fingers lost their grip. I watched in horror as the socket wrench clattered onto the brick street as if in slow motion. When Brady got out of his patrol car, my heart nearly came out of my mouth.

No, no no!

"Go try the ignition again," Brady said coolly as he bent down beside me and picked up the wrench. "I'll hit the solenoid if it won't start."

"Uh ... thanks." If I'd had a tail, it would've been tucked between my legs. "Sorry if I scratched your truck."

"Seriously?" Brady shook his head. "That's the best apology you've got?"

My mouth fell open. "What else should I—"

But Brady wasn't having it. He just stared at the engine. "Go give the ignition another turn so we can both get out of here. Okay?"

I nodded, and slunk back into the driver's seat. I tried the key. The traitorous Kia purred to life like a newborn kitten.

"You ladies really should consider getting a new vehicle," Brady said, his handsomely stern visage appearing beside Aunt Edna's window. He handed my aunt the socket wrench.

"Right you are, Officer Brady," Aunt Edna said. "Now all we need is the money to buy one. Maybe we'll get lucky and it'll fall out of the sky."

I held my breath.

Along with a meteor, please. A giant one.

Brady smiled and gently slapped the bottom of Aunt Edna's window with his palm, as if to put an end to the conversation. "Now you all please, try to stay out of trouble, would you?"

"We will!" Kitty gushed. "Thank you, Officer Brady!"

Brady's eyes met mine as if to say, "Especially *you*." I looked away, shifted into drive, and hit the gas, leaving him in a belch of black smoke.

"Whew!" Kitty said. "Good thing you didn't use that socket wrench on Eddie, or you'd be on your way to jail right now, Doreen."

"Yeah," Aunt Edna said. "And good thing Jackie wasn't with us, or we'd all be heading straight for the slammer." Aunt Edna locked eyes with me. "You remember the way to Morty's Bakery, don't you Dorey?"

I nodded. "Yes."

"Good. I'm gonna count rosary beads until we get there."

"Why? You didn't do anything wrong."

"I aided and abetted, Dorey. I threw out the empty wine bottle Jackie found under your bed. I washed all them red stains out of your shirt."

I shook my head. "But that was just wine."

"Don't you get it?" Kitty said. "You went pulled another Sammy on us, Doreen. You know, like when you got drunk and killed Tad Longmire."

"What?" I gasped. "No I didn't!"

Did I?

Chapter Twenty-Four

I pulled the old Kia into the parking lot of a run-down strip center, then found a spot near the storefront window emblazoned with the words, *Morty's Bakery*.

"Let me do the talking," Aunt Edna said, grabbing her pocketbook and opening the passenger door. "You've already dug a deep enough hole for yourself."

"Yes, Capo," I said.

Aunt Edna shot me some side eye. "That had better be sincere. You're gonna need every friend you got on this one, Dorey."

"She's right, young lady," Kitty said. "Things aren't looking to bright for you, Sunshine."

• • • •

"AND THAT'S WHEN WE spotted the body in the car," Aunt Edna said as the four of us stood in the back room of Morty's Bakery.

By this point, I was so bewildered I had no problem keeping my mouth shut. Worried that I'd actually killed Eddie in a drunken rage, neither my mouth nor my brain were in working order.

"Well, technically, *I* was the one who found him," Kitty said. "While I was clipping the azaleas, I spotted blood stains at the bottom of the Nissan's driver's door. Hard to miss against that godawful lime-green chassis."

"What time was that?" Morty asked, pulling a little red book out of his front pocket. He eyed me up and down, but didn't say a word about my trashy hair, makeup, or skin-tight jeans. No wonder he was the consigliere. The man was a pro.

"Sometime between 10:00 and 10:30, I think," Kitty said.

Aunt Edna nodded. "Sounds right. It couldn't have been more than half an hour after Dorey here told us she was hitting the mattresses, and her first "appointment" was with Eddie Houser."

Morty glanced at me. His bushy eyebrows ticked up a notch. "The girl works quick."

"Maybe, but not *that* quick," Kitty said. "From the looks of the stiff, I'd say he'd been there at least overnight. Maybe longer."

Morty exhaled through his big, red nose. "You saw the body then, Kitty. You sure it was Eddie?"

Kitty nodded. "Yeah. But not by his ugly mug. After Doreen here got done with him, his own mother wouldn't recognize him."

"So how do you know it was Eddie?" Morty asked, scratching his head with a meaty finger.

"I'll show you how." Kitty popped on some pink rubber gloves and opened the black garbage bag lying on the counter. "Take a look for yourself."

"A bloody baseball bat?" Morty frowned. "What? You already run the DNA or something?"

"No. Better." Kitty turned the bat an inch. "Look closer."

Morty squinted through his bifocals, then shook his head. "I'll be."

I stepped forward for a closer look myself. There, imbedded in the head of the baseball bat was a shiny hunk of gold. My knees began to knock.

"Looks like Eddie's eyetooth, all right," Morty said. "Okay, so the body's his." He turned to me, his eyes angry and suspicious. "Why'd you do it?"

"Go easy on her," Aunt Edna said. "She was sloppy, yeah. But this is her first job for the Family."

I burst into tears. "I didn't do it! I swear!"

Aunt Edna wrapped an arm around me. "Morty, we think our girl pulled a Sammy. She got drunk and can't remember a thing. Jackie found the baseball bat in the trunk of the Kia. She could've been driving around with it for days."

Morty shook his head. "Geez."

"I also found this beside the body," Kitty said, shoving some papers at Morty.

He grabbed them and flipped through them. "What is all this?"

"A contract," Kitty said. "Doreen did a commercial for Eddie's car lot. He was trying to sell her that Nissan Cube for a discount, instead of giving her five percent of the profits like he promised."

Morty locked eyes with me. "That tick you off, Doreen?"

I shook my head wildly. "No. I didn't even know about the contract. This is the first time I've heard of it. I swear!"

"You seem to swear a lot," Morty said, taking off his bifocals.

I cringed. "I didn't kill Eddie, I swea ..."

"What if the kid isn't lying," Kitty asked. "If you ask me, she's too smart to be driving around with the murder weapon."

"Unless she didn't remember nothing about it," Aunt Edna said.

"Or somebody planted it on her," Kitty said.

Morty rubbed his eyes. "Well, if *she* didn't kill Eddie, who did?"

"Maybe it was a message job from Humpty," Kitty said.

"A message job?" I asked.

Kitty nodded. "Yeah. You know. A bullet in the mouth sends the message that you talk too much. A bullet in the eye, you saw too much. A bullet to the groin—"

"I get it," I said. "But whoever killed Eddie didn't use bullets."

"No, they used that thing right there," Morty said, nodding toward the bloody baseball bat.

"So, what kind of message could that mean?" I asked.

"Besides that *you* did it?" Morty said.

I cringed. "Yes. Besides that."

Morty eyed me up and down. "Maybe it was Sammy saying it's your turn at bat."

My eyes grew wide. "What?"

"Or maybe it was his way of warning Humpty to keep away from his girl," Aunt Edna said.

Kitty nodded. "Like father, like daughter."

I suddenly felt the world closing in on me "What are you saying?"

Aunt Edna laid a hand on my shoulder. "I didn't want you to find out this way, Dorey, but Sammy's your father."

Chapter Twenty-Five

I now knew how Luke Skywalker felt—but I didn't have *The Force* behind me. I had *The Family.*

Sammy the Psycho is my father? This can't be happening!

The backroom of Morty's Bakery began to spin. I wobbled on my stilettos. I was about to keel over when Aunt Edna caught me by the arm.

"Steady, Dorey."

I shook my head in dismay. "Is that why my mother hated me?"

"Maureen didn't hate you Dorey." Aunt Edna patted my arm. "She just kept a little distant. She had her reasons."

"And now she's disappeared," I said.

Aunt Edna nodded. "Maureen's in the wind."

I moaned, and burst into tears. "Sammy killed her!"

"No, Hun," Kitty said. "You got it all wrong. Maureen's where she always wanted to be. She's *with Sammy*."

"What?" I sniffed. "Why? How? Where are they?"

"We can't tell you, because nobody knows," Aunt Edna said. "And nobody will, unless they want us to. Doreen, you've got to understand something. Don't believe everything you hear about Sammy, okay?"

"What do you mean?"

"I can't say. Only that Sammy and your ma waited forty years to be together. Who are we to deny them their chance at happiness?"

"But why did they have to wait?" I asked.

"For a lot of reasons," Morty said. "But we ain't got time for that now."

"The biggest reason was they were waiting for you to come into your own," Aunt Edna said, putting an arm around my waist.

"Come into my own?" I gasped. "You mean, be a killer like Sammy?"

"Yeah," Morty said.

"But I *can't* be!" I squealed. "Before I came here, nothing like this ever happened to me!"

"It takes women more time to gather up enough rage at the world to turn homicidal," Kitty said. "That's a proven fact. Why else would most serial killers be men?"

"Yeah, blame it on the men," Morty said sourly. "It's always *our* fault."

"Look, Morty," Aunt Edna said. "We came to you for advice. So give us some!"

"Okay, fine." Morty opened his little red book. "Where's the car? We've got to get rid of it."

"In front of our place," Aunt Edna said.

Morty nodded, and ran an index finger down a page in the book. "Okay, I'll call my cousin at the scrapyard."

"Thanks, Morty." Aunt Edna nodded toward the bat. "And could you get rid of that?"

"Yeah." Morty sighed. "I'll put some feelers out, too. See who knows what about what's already gone down."

"We've got to keep a close eye on Humpty," I said. "He's got to be involved in this somehow."

Aunt Edna nodded. "Doreen thinks Humpty was in on that scheme to poison Sophia on her birthday. Maybe he's tired of skimming off the Family Fund and wants to get his hands on the whole wad."

"I wouldn't put it past him," Morty said. "I never have liked that guy. I'll put a tail on him."

"Thanks, Morty" I said. I broke free of my aunt and Kitty and hugged him. He patted my back stiffly, then pushed me away.

"Now for Pete's sake," he said. "You ladies go home and lock your windows and doors."

"Why?" I asked.

He scowled at me. "Because when you start hitting the mattresses, Dorey, *everybody's* a target."

• • • •

ON THE DRIVE HOME, Aunt Edna kept glancing in the side-view mirror.

"Anybody tailing us?" Kitty asked.

"No. Not yet, anyway," Aunt Edna said.

"We've got to find the real killer," I said. "Why didn't you mention the coffee, Aunt Edna?"

"Because there's nothing to tell," she said. "Kitty said it wasn't poisoned. And Sophia swore you to secrecy about it. There's no need to let Sophia know we're on to her. If she knew we knew, no telling what kind of 'chores' she might have in store for you."

"Oh. Thanks."

"You really think I killed Eddie?" I asked.

"It don't matter either way, Dorey. You're Family. If you did it, you did it for *us*. We love you no matter what."

A lump the size of an egg pressed down on my tonsils. I couldn't speak. When Aunt Edna reached over and gently patted my thigh, it was all I could do not to break down and sob.

Chapter Twenty-Six

"That was Morty on the phone," Aunt Edna said, tucking her cellphone back into the big, brown pocketbook on her lap. She turned and glanced at Kitty in the backseat of the Kia. "The guy with the tow truck is on his way."

Kitty nodded. "Let's hope he gets there before the cops do."

Aunt Edna touched my arm. "Better step on it, Dorey."

"Yes, ma'am."

Speeding down Fourth Street toward Palm Court Cottages, my mind swirled with a mishmash of contradicting thoughts. What *really had* happened to Eddie? Had I clubbed him to death in a drunken rage? Or had someone else beaten me to it?

Maybe it was one of those angry women with picket signs. Or an old customer Eddie had swindled. Perhaps his wife Kareena? There certainly hadn't seemed to be any love-loss there.

Or maybe it really *was* me.

Drunken Doreen in the Nissan Cube with a baseball bat.

As I passed an old man at a bus stop in shorts and a wife-beater T-shirt, the thought of being back in LA clipping Arthur Dreacher's toenails began to take on a certain allure ...

"I'm telling you, you can't convict without a body," Aunt Edna's voice burst through my thought bubble. How long she and Kitty had been arguing, I couldn't say.

"Sure you can," Kitty said. "It's just a little harder, that's all. DNA evidence is the new smoking gun. It's like the hand of God pointing a finger right at you."

"Even so, I'm glad the body's gone," Aunt Edna said. "*And* the bat. Once the blasted car is off our street, we're home free."

"And there it goes now," Kitty said, pointing toward a tow truck passing us in the opposite lane. The rig was hauling a lime-green, cube-shaped car. The driver shot us a thumb's up as he sped by.

While I watched the Nissan on the tow truck disappear in the rearview mirror, a boulder lifted off my shoulders.

I didn't know if that was a good sign, or a bad one.

The only thing I knew for sure was, I was in this mess up to my ultra-teased hairline.

AS I TURNED ONTO THE street in front of Palm Court Cottages, an avalanche of boulders fell back on top of my shoulders.

A cop car and a forensics van was parked right in front of the apartments.

I recognized the cop—a tall, slim, black man. He was none other than Sergeant McNulty. My molars pressed together. Sergeant McNulty had it out for me. Every time I turned up next to a dead body, he blamed me. Go figure?

I cringed. "Aww, crap."

"McNutsack," Aunt Edna muttered. "This ain't good."

"Stay calm," Kitty said, putting a hand on my shoulder from the backseat. "Just keep driving like nothing's happening."

I tried to do as Kitty commanded, but people were everywhere. Onlookers lined the streets, pointing and gawking at something in front of the apartments.

"What are they looking at?" I asked.

"I dunno," Kitty said. "Something by the curb."

"Keep going," Aunt Edna said. "We're almost to his car."

Slowly, I cautiously steered the Kia, weaving through the crowded scene at a snail's pace. As we passed McNulty's police car, I was about to breathe a sigh of relief when a fat guy in gym shorts and a T-shirt started crossing the road right in front of us. He couldn't have walked slower if he were going backward.

"Geez. Of all the luck," I grumbled, nervously chewing my bottom lip as the guy slowly blundered along. Just as he reached the center of the road, he dropped his water bottle. He bent over to pick it up, lost his balance, and toppled over head first onto the brick street.

"Ouch," I said. "Should I go help him?"

"No. Stay in the car!" Aunt Edna hissed. "Don't worry about him. Don't look like he uses that head of his much, anyway."

Time seemed to stand still as we held our breath and watched the guy slowly grunt and huff his way to his feet. It was then I noticed he had a cleft chin.

Seriously, Doreen? Maybe Aunt Edna's right. I'm as looney-toons as my father.

"He's clear," Kitty said. "Punch it!"

"Right." I was about to hit the gas when a pair of knuckles banged on the window right by my head. I turned and felt a quarter of my life-force drain away.

"Diller, is that you?" McNulty asked.

I glanced in the mirror at my candy-apple lips, bozo hair, and fake beauty mark. "Yes. Unfortunately, it's me," I muttered under my breath.

"Roll down your window," McNulty demanded. "Where are you going?"

My guilty brain curdled like cottage cheese. "Um ... just ... yeah. You know."

McNulty lowered his mirrored sunglasses and glared at me. "No, I *don't* know, Diller, or I wouldn't be asking."

"We're looking for a parking space, officer McNut ... uh," Aunt Edna said.

"What's going on, officer?" Kitty blurted.

"Big pool of blood by the curb," McNulty said. "You ladies know anything about it?"

"No, sir," Kitty said.

"Aww, for the love of," Aunt Edna hissed.

I turned away from McNulty toward Aunt Edna. She was staring out the passenger window toward the apartments. Suddenly, I saw what she saw.

Jackie was hoofing it down the garden path toward us. Still dressed in that blazing red shirt and green pants, she kept dragging a boney finger across her chicken-neck throat like a doomed member of a *Star Trek* landing party.

"Real subtle, that one," Kitty muttered, then slumped back into her seat.

By some Christmas-in-June miracle, McNulty apparently hadn't noticed Jackie. He continued his line of questioning. "So you're saying you don't know nothing about the blood on the curb?"

"Did an animal get hit by a car?" I asked.

"Don't know yet." McNulty glanced around inside our vehicle. "But I have reason to believe it's more serious than that."

"You do?" I said, trying not to squeal.

"Yes, I do." McNulty pulled out his cellphone. "Someone called in an anonymous tip about the blood being human. Then I received this video."

I gulped. "Video?"

McNulty shoved his cellphone in my face. Playing on the display was an outtake from the commercial I shot with Kerri at Crazy Eddie's Used Car Lot.

There I was, in the same Daisy the Price Slayer outfit I was donning yet again today. I watched the screen as I swung that stupid rubber sword and accidently hit Eddie in the neck with it. Eddie grasped his throat and fell backward. The video cut off.

I groaned inside. It had all been a joke. But it appeared Eddie was going to have the last laugh.

"That was just us goofing around at a commercial shoot on Wednesday," I said.

"Is that so." McNulty eyed me, then Aunt Edna and Kitty. "Can anyone corroborate your story?"

I nodded. "Yes, sir. Kerri and Marshall at—"

"I can," Jackie said. She jutted her pointy chin at McNulty. "That clip there is totally bogus. Everybody knows that ain't the way Houser got whacked."

Chapter Twenty-Seven

"So, just exactly how *did* Eddie Houser 'get whacked?'" McNulty asked Jackie. He held a pen to his notepad, ready to record the moment our ship was torpedoed.

I groaned, already hearing the handcuffs clinking shut around my wrists. As I awaited my inevitable incarceration, Aunt Edna grabbed a life raft and started bailing.

"Jackie, you been watching too much TV again," my aunt said, climbing out of the car. "Sorry, officer. The old gal's got dementia. She's always getting Eddie Houser mixed up with *Doogie Howser, M.D.*" She elbowed Jackie in the ribs. "Ain't that right, Jackie?"

"Uh ...," Jackie said. Unable to lie, her narrow face creased with confusion. Apparently, Jackie still didn't realize she'd just spilled a pot of baked beans big enough to bury us all the way to Boston.

"See, officer?" Aunt Edna said, shaking her head. "Just look at that dumb, confused expression. She definitely forgot to take her meds again this morning."

"I mean, who in their right mind would wear that outfit?" Kitty said, climbing out of the backseat. She took Jackie's other elbow. "She thinks she's an elf. We better get her back into her apartment before she wanders off again."

"Yeah," Aunt Edna said, and started tugging on Jackie's elbow.

"Hold on," McNulty said.

Kitty winked at him and whispered, "Yesterday, she kept asking where Pat was. She thought she was Vanna White. We better get her inside. Those diapers aren't getting any fresher, if you catch my drift."

A horn honked behind us. The Kia was blocking the street.

"Fine, go," McNulty said. "But Diller, get your car out of the street. Then you and I need to talk."

••••

I LED MCNULTY BEYOND the prying eyes of the crowd on the street, over to the picnic table in the center of the tropical courtyard. Aunt Edna had offered to bring us iced tea, but I was glad when McNulty turned her down. All we needed was to have another body to get rid of.

"Play the video again," I asked McNulty. "I want to show you something."

He plucked his phone from his breast pocket and loaded the video.

"Take a good look," I said. "You can see in the background that the video was filmed at the car lot. Like I tried to explain earlier, I can get Kerri and Marshall at Sunshine City Studios to send you the rest of the clip. You'll see Eddie Houser was just pulling a prank on me. I swear, he was alive and kicking when I left the lot."

McNulty tucked his phone back into his pocket. "Why would he pull a prank like that?" He crossed his arms and studied me like a puzzle he was trying to figure out.

"Because he's a jer ... Jersey native, I think. Pranking is in their blood."

"Uh-huh. Speaking of which, if that blood on the curb turns out to belong to Eddie Houser, you can bet I'll be back here before you can say 'Jersey Devil.'"

"Yes, sir."

McNulty's phone rang. He took the call. "I see," he said, then hung up. "Well, the blood on the curb is no mutt's. It's human."

I gasped. It was no act.

"You don't mind if we search your premises, do you," McNulty said. It wasn't a question.

My heart began humping in my throat. "No. Of course not."

"Good. I'll send a couple of officers out now."

• • • •

I BARELY HAD TIME TO get out of the Daisy Duke Jeans of Death and scrub the makeup off my face before I heard a knock at the door.

"Remember what we talked about," Aunt Edna said. "There ain't no evidence inside the house. So there's nothing to worry about."

"Right." I chewed my thumbnail. "Nothing to worry about, except the trunk of the Kia where the bloody bat was."

Aunt Edna patted me on the shoulder. "Don't worry! We're gonna make the Kia disappear during the search."

"Then you better get going." I handed her the keys.

"Leaving now. Out the back door."

"Be sure and get Jackie out of here, too," I whispered.

Aunt Edna shot me a look. "You think this is my first rodeo? Now relax. Breathe. You got this, Dorey."

I nodded. "Okay. I'll call you when the coast is clear."

The knock sounded at the door again.

Aunt Edna patted me on the shoulder, then turned and headed through the kitchen toward the back door.

Calling on everything I'd learned from years of acting classes, I prepared for the performance of a lifetime. , Channeling my inner Doris Day, I smoothed my hair and dress, then plastered on a smile and opened the door.

"Diller?" the cop said.

Doris caught a cab to a liquor store.

I glared at the cop. "Brady. Why did McNulty send *you* to search our place? Isn't this some kind of conflict of interest or something?"

"Why would it be?" Brady said. "I have no personal interests here."

And with that bullet to the heart, I stepped aside and let him in.

Chapter Twenty-Eight

While Brady ransacked my aunt's apartment, I flopped into the Barcalounger and surfed the internet for cheap ways out of the country. On Craig's list, some guy named Lefty was looking for a cook to serve on a junket cruise down to Bogota and back.

What the hell? My goose is probably cooked, anyway.

I was about to type Lefty an email when Brady shouted out my name.

"Diller! Bedroom!"

If only...

I hauled my butt out of the chair and padded to my bedroom.

"What's this?" Brady asked, holding up my leather journal.

"That's personal!" I said, then scrambled to snatch it out of his hands. "It was a birthday gift from Kitty!"

Brady held the book over his head, out of my reach. "Sit down, Diller."

My face as hot as the surface of the sun, I flopped onto the edge of the bed and crossed my arms. "What?"

Brady opened the journal and read from it aloud. "Humpty Bogart has a cleft chin?"

"Yes," I huffed. "I tried to tell you that the other night."

"I thought you were making it up," Brady said. "Humpty Bogart?"

"It's a nickname for Humphrey Bogaratelli." My shoulders slumped. "But it doesn't matter anymore. Turns out, every Tom, Dick, and Harry in St. Pete has a cleft chin."

"Who's Bogaratelli?"

I frowned.

A slimy bagman bilking the Collard Green Cosa Nostra out of their ill-gotten gains.

"He's a money manager for my aunt," I said. "I thought he might be involved with Montoya in trying to poison Sophia, okay?"

"Why didn't you tell me?"

"I tried! But you were too busy laughing at me about it."

"Laughing at you? I didn't."

"You asked me if Humpty Bogart was the father of Monkey-Faced Mongo. Remember?"

Brady frowned. "I thought it was Mongo the Monkey Boy."

"Whatever! Can I have my journal back now, please?" I made a grab for the notebook. Brady was quicker.

"Not so fast." Brady turned a page in the journal and started reading aloud. "What's wrong with Brady? Forty and not married. Some kind of power-hungry perv? What a baby, getting all pissed at me over a scratch on his bumper! Any man who loves his truck more than me can go to—"

"I wrote that in a moment of anger!" I blurted.

"So that's why you defaced my truck? You think I'm a power-hungry pervert?"

I closed my eyes and tried to clear my head. At this point, my mouth was a shovel, busily digging my grave. I opened my eyes and said, "I don't want to talk about it. You said this wasn't personal."

Brady shook his head and snapped the journal shut. "Geez, Diller. This is my payback for not laughing at your joke? You're a real hothead. Especially when you've been drinking. My advice? Don't drink anymore. And don't date."

• • • •

RELEGATED TO THE BARCALOUNGER while Brady finished his search of my aunt's cottage, I pecked out a note to Lefty on my laptop. I was about to press *send* when Brady called my name again.

"Diller! Laundry room."

I set down my laptop and dragged myself to the small nook off the kitchen that housed the washer and dryer. Brady was standing there holding a pair of sopping-wet jeans.

The Daisy Duke jeans. Aunt Edna must've tossed them into the wash.

"Are these yours?" he asked.

"Well, yes. But technically they belong to the Studio."

"Why are you washing your clothes now, during a police search? In my line of work, this is called trying to get rid of evidence."

"Seriously?" I scowled. "I voluntarily submitted to this search, remember? In my line of work, that's what we call Friday night laundry. Why are you persecuting me, Brady?"

"I'm not persecuting you. I'm trying to help you."

My eyebrows rose and inch. "Help me? By *incriminating* me?"

"Look, Doreen. I asked for the assignment to search your place."

"Why?"

"Because you have this uncanny knack for incriminating *yourself*. I thought I could shield you. Listen to your explanations and sort things out." He looked down at the sopping jeans. "But even *I* find this hard to explain away."

"Size six jeans?"

"No. The bloody fingerprint on the back left thigh."

"What?" I gasped. "It's ... it's probably just ketchup from a corndog."

"Seriously?" Brady shook his head. "That's the best excuse you can come up with?"

"But—"

"I'm going to have to take these in evidence." Brady slipped the jeans into a plastic bag. "You'd better pray this isn't blood. And that if it is, you better pray even harder that it doesn't match that pool of blood on the curb outside."

At a loss for words, I simply nodded.

"And Doreen? Don't go anywhere. As of this moment, I'm having McNulty place you under house arrest."

Chapter Twenty-Nine

"The coast is clear," I said into my cellphone as I peeked through the living room curtains. Officer Brady was leaving down the courtyard path.

"Good," Aunt Edna said. "It's too late to get dinner started. We're picking up takeout on the way home. You got a hankering for anything?"

Yeah. A fast boat to China.

I sighed. "How about Chinese?"

"You got it. See you in a bit."

"No hurry. Believe me, I'm not going anywhere."

I hung up the phone and flopped into "the good chair." Utterly dejected, it occurred to me that somehow I'd managed to star in a 3-D disaster movie of my own making.

One—the disastrous *date* with Brady. Two—the disastrous *death* of Crazy Eddie. And three—my disastrous fate as the *daughter* of Sammy the psycho.

I shook my head in disbelief. My whole Family thought I was a next-generation psycho killer. Even worse, I was seriously beginning to think they might be right. I'd have asked the Universe what else could possibly go wrong, but as of late I'd come to believe that was a trick question ...

• • • •

"YOU'VE HARDLY TOUCHED your Peking Duck," Aunt Edna said as we sat around the dining room table digging through cardboard cartons from Lucky Duck Chinese Restaurant. "What's wrong?"

"Maybe it's because I feel like a *sitting* duck," I said, picking at my food with a pair of chopsticks. "Now even *Brady* thinks I killed Eddie."

Aunt Edna frowned. "Huh. Brady's always been on our side."

"That's because up to now, we haven't gotten our hands this dirty," Kitty said.

Jackie examined her fingernails. "My hands ain't dirty. I used Lysol."

I glanced from face to face at each of the three little old ladies who'd worked so hard to cover a killer's tracks—possibly *my* tracks. They didn't deserve this mess.

I pushed my chair back and stood up. "Thanks for all your help, ladies. But I'm not hungry. I need to be alone for a while."

"You go ahead, Dorey," Aunt Edna said. "We'll be here for you when you're ready to talk."

I nodded. "Thanks."

As I turned to go, a knock sounded at the front door.

"I'll get it," I said. "I'm already up."

"If it's the cops, don't let them in without a warrant," Kitty said.

"Right." I headed for the front door and yanked it open, ready to deliver a speech about our rights as citizens of the United States. But to my surprise, no one was there. Instead, a bouquet of white flowers lay on the doormat.

"Relax! It's just flowers," I called out, then picked them up and carried them into the dining room.

"Who're they for?" Jackie asked. She elbowed Aunt Edna. "Maybe they're from one of your 'pen pals.'"

"Can it," Aunt Edna grumbled.

"What's the card say?" Kitty asked.

I set the flowers on the table and plucked the small envelope from the plastic pick poking from the bouquet. I opened it, swallowed hard, and read the handwritten note out loud.

"It says, 'You're dead to me.'"

Chapter Thirty

"Who could've sent the flowers?" I asked, staring wide-eyed at the trio of elderly mob molls.

"Monkey-Face Mongo?" Jackie asked, ribbing Aunt Edna.

Aunt Edna winced. "Crap. I forgot about him."

I chewed my bottom lip. "Do you think he might have tracked you down to get his money back? Or *worse*?"

Aunt Edna shook her head. "Marco Telleroni ain't the brightest bulb in the box. Still, he *is* a made man, so he's bona fide to make a hit."

"You think he killed Eddie?" I asked.

"I was thinking more like him wanting to kill me," Aunt Edna said. "But Marco would send a message first. You know, to let me know he was on to me."

I waved the note in the air. "And you don't think 'You're dead to me.' is a message?"

"It's a message, all right." Aunt Edna took the note from me and studied it. "But it probably ain't Marco. All the words are spelled right."

"Somebody else could've written it for him," Kitty said.

"Maybe." Aunt Edna glanced around at each of us. "But these flowers could've just as easily come from Humpty Bogart for Sophia."

"How do you figure that?" Jackie asked.

"Maybe he's trying to scare her into a heart attack or something, since the poison didn't work."

"We're not even sure it's Humpty trying to poison her, or if *anybody* is at this point," I said.

"Then who?" Kitty asked.

I grimaced. "Brady. He made it pretty clear this afternoon that our relationship was dead in the water."

"Brady?" Aunt Edna said. "Nah. I can't believe that."

"What about Eddie's family?" Kitty asked. "They could've sent them. They probably heard it through the grapevine by now."

"Heard what?" I asked.

"That you started a clan war and killed Eddie," Kitty said.

I winced. "How would they have heard about that?"

Aunt Edna and Kitty's eyes darted toward Jackie.

"Why you lookin' at me?" Jackie said. "I didn't tell nobody nothing." She made a sour face and pulled the shoulder of her red shirt. Elves don't gossip. Even Santa knows that."

"These flowers are white chrysanthemums," I said, picking up the bouquet. "Kitty, what do those mean?"

Kitty shook her head. "What do you think, Dorey? They mean *death*."

"Oh." My already clattering heart fell to my knees. I felt dizzy and nauseated.

"You okay?" Kitty asked.

"Yes. Uh ... I'm going to my room for a while. I need to rethink my life while I've still got a life to rethink."

• • • •

I SAT ON THE EDGE OF my bed and stared at the cardboard boxes stacked against the wall. It was hard to believe only three days had passed since the cartons containing my old life back in LA had arrived on Aunt Edna's doorstep. With everything going haywire around me, I hadn't had time to unpack them.

I frowned and wondered what Sonya, my old roommate back in South Park, was up to. We'd both been grunts at a Hollywood production studio.

A smile curled my lips as I imagined Sonya running around like mad, trying to appease whichever celebrity dictator she'd been assigned to tonight. I envisioned her trying to catch a fitful nap in a dirty cot in the corner of the production studio. I could almost hear Sonya grunting as she squeezed a witchy prima donna into full-body Spanx ...

I sighed with envy. That ship had sailed. My eyes focused back on the boxes against the wall.

At least when I go to prison, I won't have to repack.

On that cheery note, I got up off my duff and picked up the package from my mother. I'd opened it on my birthday three days ago, hoping she'd sent me a gift. Instead, the box had been crammed with my baby pictures and childhood stuff.

Junk Ma didn't want anymore.

Like a stupid moth to a flame, I opened the box again. Lying atop the pile of painful memories was a picture of me and Ma in a park outside Snohomish.

My heart burned with anger and pain as Aunt Edna's words sounded in my head. "Your ma and Sammy waited forty years to be together. Who are we to deny them their chance at happiness?"

What about my *happiness? Didn't you care about me at all, Ma?*

Rage surged through me. I hurled the box against the wall. Photos, toys, eyepatches, and junk scattered everywhere.

I shook my head. I'd just created yet *another* mess I had to clean up.

Good going, Doreen.

Limp with hopelessness, I bent down and picked up the empty box. As I started tossing stuff back into it, a flash of color caught my eye.

An envelope had been taped to the inside bottom of the box.

A teal-colored envelope labeled, *To Doreen.*

Chapter Thirty-One

Dear Doreen,

By now, you know the truth. Sammy Lorenzo is your father. I'm sorry I didn't tell you earlier, but I had my reasons. Before you hate me for it, please give me a chance to explain.

Harvey Lorenzo (Sophia's husband) had big plans for his sons, Saul and Samuel. Saul towed the line. But Sammy had plans of his own.

He and I fell in love. Harvey bitterly disapproved of me. I wasn't the mob moll darling he had in mind for Sammy. But by the time Harvey put the hammer down, you'd already been conceived.

Harvey was as brutal as he was handsome. He threatened to do Sammy in. He started spreading lies about Sammy being a drunk and a rage killer. But his scheme backfired. Instead of ruining Sammy, his reputation only grew.

Everyone began to fear Sammy more than they feared Harvey. And in the Family, fear is the same thing as respect. Harvey became enraged and obsessed with punishing Sammy for making a fool out of him—even though he'd done the dirty work himself.

Sammy had no choice but to disappear. And that meant you and I had to, as well. Sammy didn't want us to live in fear of the mob coming after us. So before I started showing and Harvey put two and two together, Sammy set us up in that house in Snohomish, as far away from Florida as we could get.

The plan was for Sammy to go to Wisconsin and work as a mechanic until things cooled off. But they never cooled off. Rumors started to spread that Sammy had gone rogue and joined a rival Family. The truth was, all Sammy wanted was a peaceful life for the three of us. But Harvey wouldn't let him go.

When you were about to turn four years old, Sammy wrote me saying he thought he'd been found out. Not long afterward, Sammy sent me a newspaper clipping about Harvey and Saul dying in a car accident near Manitowoc.

Doreen, Harvey and Saul had been hunting for Sammy. To exterminate him.

I don't know if the car crash was really an accident or not. Sammy never told me, and to be honest, I never asked. I didn't want to know. If Sammy killed his father and brother, it was to save us. So how can I hold it against him?

After the accident, RICO agents really turned up the heat on mafia families. The campaign to get Sammy got shoved to the back burner. But believe me, there are still people who hold grudges out there, running free.

Sammy feels it's still not safe to show his face, much less mine. If he did, it might stir up things again. People might want to reopen the accident investigation. Who knows what they'd uncover with today's technology? I don't want to take the risk—for your sake, and Sammy's.

Thankfully, as far as I know, Harvey and Sophia never found out about you. I only told Edna. My dear sister put her life on the line for us. She invented a cover story about me getting a job and moving to Detroit. She also kept the story alive about Sammy being a killer, so people would be afraid to go after him and find us in the process.

Edna's never wavered from her story. Ever. Don't ask her to, Doreen. She'll tell you when the she feels the time is right.

I never told you any of this before because I didn't want you to get caught up in the Lorenzo "Family business." At least, not until you were old enough and wise enough to decide for yourself what you wanted. And you are now.

I've watched you come into your own, Dorey. And I'm proud to say you're the most determined, persistent, and irascible person I've ever known—except maybe for your father. And Sammy's just as proud of you as I am. I thought you should know.

Now for the hard part. Doreen, I know I didn't show you the kind of love you deserved. But you have to understand, I lived in constant fear that Sophia would find out about you and take you away from me. You were like a present I couldn't keep.

As a result, I'll admit I never really bonded the way I should have with you. I shielded my heart for fear of it breaking when they finally took you away. It was wrong. I know that now. And even though they never found us, I fear you got damaged in the process anyway. That's my fault. And I'm sorrier about it than I can express here.

Sammy and I stayed apart for forty years to protect you. He worked hard to pay for you and me to live in isolation. I hope the sacrifice we both made shows you how much you mean to us.

But time isn't on our side any longer. We're both getting old. We knew if we didn't get together now, well, maybe we never would. And what would be the point of living any longer?

Then, when you called me to say you were in St. Petersburg, Florida, you were practically on Edna's doorstep. I took it as a sign, Doreen. And now, with you living there with Edna, I'm not worried so much anymore. Not about Sophia or the mob coming after me and Sammy, anyway.

But let me warn you of this: If Sophia figures out her niece is actually Sammy's daughter, there's no telling what might happen. I believe she, like a lot of people, blames Sammy for Harvey and Saul's death. And as I've explained, the need for revenge runs deep with the Lorenzos.

I can't help you with money or muscle, Doreen. Sammy and I have little of either. But we can give you our love. And one other thing—leverage. Two secrets I've kept safe for forty years. With Sammy at my side, I've got all the protection I need now. So I'm passing them on to you.

My darling daughter, it's totally your call how to use this information. Just remember, whatever you do, I'll always love you, no matter what. And so will Sammy.

Be brave,

Ma

I turned to the next page of Ma's letter and gasped.

I wasn't exactly sure what to do with the information she'd just given me. But thanks to Ma, I'd just been forewarned—and fore*armed*.

Chapter Thirty-Two

As I re-read my mother's letter, the missing pieces to my life—and my heart—began to fill themselves in.

I felt like the *Grinch* when his heart suddenly grew 10,000 times bigger. I felt like James Garner in *The Notebook*, when his wife finally recognized who he was. I felt like Julia Roberts in *Erin Brockovich*, when she got fed up with all the bull-crap in the world and started kicking people's butts.

I'd swear I actually felt my spine grow stronger.

I'm tired of always paying the price but never getting any of the glory. I'm sick to death of being at the whim of other people!

I folded the precious letter and tucked it into my shirt pocket. Fortified with Ma's pure love and her dirty secrets, I was no longer willing to cower in a corner and wait for the world to strike me down.

"Meteors be damned!" I said, and marched straight back to the dining room.

"You hungry now?" Aunt Edna asked. "We saved you some egg rolls."

"No. I want something else."

"What?" Aunt Edna asked. "Linguini?"

I crossed my arms and straightened my shoulders. "An Omertà. What I'm about to say doesn't leave this room. Capeesh?"

"Sure, Dorey," Aunt Edna said. "You okay with that, ladies?"

Jackie and Kitty nodded.

"Good." I locked eyes with Aunt Edna. "I want you to call Morty and invite him to breakfast tomorrow morning at six o'clock sharp."

"What for?" Kitty asked.

"Because," I said defiantly. "We're going to start beating the mattresses again. *For real* this time."

Aunt Edna choked on a mouthful of chow Mein. "Are you serious?"

I gave her one short nod. "Yes. *Dead* serious."

"Uh, who died and left you in charge?" Jackie asked, pointing a chopstick at me.

I shot her my best evil grin. "Nobody. *Yet*. But the first person on my list is Doña Sophia Maria Lorenzo."

Chapter Thirty-Three

It was 5:25 a.m. I was standing in the dark courtyard in front of Sophia's apartment, waiting on cute, hoodie-headed Mr. ScarBux to arrive.

As part of my plan, I'd figured I should stick to the routine, so Sophia wouldn't get suspicious. But little did she know, delivering her coffee was the last grunt work I expected to ever do for the old Queenpin.

Tucked inside my shirt pocket was my ticket to freedom—and to Sophia's potential demise.

"Good morning," I said as the hooded figure drew nearer.

"Morning," he said, a smile appearing above his cleft-less chin. "Here's your order."

I handed him twelve bucks. "Thanks."

"Oh, and here's some more sugar." He reached into his jacket pocket and pulled out a plastic baggie full of sugar packets.

"A baggie full?"

Chase shrugged. "The old lady likes her sugar."

"Right." I took the packets and watched him go. I turned around and nearly swallowed my tonsils. Someone was standing in the dark a mere two feet from me.

"Jackie!" I gasped. "What are you doing up so early?"

"I wanted to see if you were really gonna murderize Sophia."

"What?"

"Death by sugar," Jackie said. "Pretty clever."

"What are you talking about?"

"Sophia's diabetic. That stuff could kill her."

"Oh." I stared at the baggie of packets. "You know what, Jackie? I've got a feeling you may be right."

Jackie shrugged. "We'll, I ain't no doctor, but I seen one on TV."

I smiled and crooked my elbow around hers. "Come with me, Sherlock."

Arm in arm, we walked the few paces over to Kitty's cottage. Jackie tapped softly on the front door. A moment later, Kitty appeared, dressed and ready for our 6 a.m. meeting, except for the pink rollers in her hair.

"What's up?" she asked.

"This," I said, holding up the baggie of packets. "If I'm right, these things are full of poison. Could you run some tests, then meet us over at Aunt Edna's?"

"Sure." She held up the packets. "ScarBux?"

"It's a new coffee joint," I said.

"Hmm," Kitty said. "I've never heard of it."

• • • •

WHILE JACKIE REPLACED the coffee in the paper ScarBux containers with fresh brew from Aunt Edna's coffee carafe, I pulled out my laptop and searched the internet.

"There's no mention of ScarBux," I said.

Jackie shrugged. "You said they were new."

"Yeah," I said. "Even so, if they went to the trouble to print cups and packets with their logo on them, they're market savvy enough to be online. Nowadays, the internet knows about everything."

Jackie cringed. Her eyes darted around the room. "*Everything*?"

"Everything. ScarBux has got to be a front. I'm sure someone really *is* trying to poison Sophia."

"You mean besides you?"

"Argh!" I groaned. "Jackie, for the millionth time, no! It's not *me*."

"Then who?" Aunt Edna asked, walking into the kitchen.

I pursed my lips. "I don't know yet. Maybe that cute little ScarBux kid isn't so cute after all."

"You want we should have somebody run him down?" Aunt Edna asked.

"No. We don't have time for that. We can lay in wait for him tomorrow. In the meantime, put another pot of coffee on. It's gonna be a long morning."

I grabbed the refilled ScarBux cups.

"I can take them to Sophia," Jackie said, tossing the used coffee filter in the garbage.

"No," I said. "I'll do it. I've got something I need to discuss with the Queenpin anyway."

Aunt Edna put a hand on my shoulder. "Listen, Dorey. She's just a little old lady."

"Don't worry. I'll be bringing her back here alive. I promise. I need her for my plan to work." I smiled. "I need *all* of you."

"What plan you talking about?" Jackie asked.

"I'll explain everything as soon as Morty gets here. I've just got one loose end to tie up first."

"Here," Jackie said, handing me a zip-tie. "Fresh from the box."

Chapter Thirty-Four

As I stepped halfway into Sophia's front door, someone reached out and snatched the bag of ScarBux coffee out of my hand. Startled out of my wits, I let loose a string of obscenities.

"You kiss your mother with that mouth?" Sophia asked, digging into the paper sack. "Where you been? You're late."

"Geez, Sophia!" I gasped. "You scared me half to death. Sorry I'm three minutes late. I was busy saving your life again."

"Oh, yeah?" she said, plucking a cup from the bag. "How can I ever thank you?"

I scowled. "How about by dying?"

Sophia snorted. "You mean like when Edna put enough Metamucil in my breakfast to blow me up?" She took a sip of coffee from the paper container. "Ugh. You switched these again." She shook her head. "You want to kill me? One more sip of this shlock and Edna will have beaten you to the punch."

Sophia shoved the sack holding the other coffee into my hands. "You know the routine," she said, then hobbled over and flopped onto the couch.

I headed for the kitchen to fetch her royal pain-in-the-Queenpin a *real* cup and saucer. When I returned, she was staring at me like a hungry lioness.

"You really want me to die, young Doreen? I knew you were ambitious. But are you really ruthless enough to bump off a defenseless old lady?"

I frowned and took the ScarBux coffee container from her gnarled hand. "I didn't mean *really* die." I transferred the coffee from the container to her ceramic cup. "I meant that I want you to *pretend* to be dead."

"Oh." Sophia scowled at the cup of coffee I handed her. "First my hair falls out. And now my taste buds are being tortured to death. What's left worth living for anyway?"

I smirked. "Go ahead. I know about the sugar."

Sophia eyed me with keen interest. "You seem to know a lot. Maybe more than you should." She reached between the sofa cushions and pulled out a baggie of ScarBux sugar packets.

"Ha! I thought so!" I snatched the baggie from her hands. "That stuff could be killing you!"

"Double crosser!" Sophia hissed. "You know something, Doreen? At my age, I don't give a flip if sugar does me in. Food is the last of life's pleasures that I've got left."

I dangled the baggie in front of her. "Are you saying you no longer have a taste for revenge?"

The old woman's thin lips curled upward. "I didn't exactly say *that*."

"Good. Hold on a moment." I walked over to the front door and opened it a crack. "Jackie?"

Jackie appeared from the shadows. "Present and accounted for."

"Take these over to Kitty." I handed her the baggie of sugar packets. "Tell her to test them separate from the others."

Jackie nodded. "You got it."

I closed the door and walked back over to Sophia. She was fiddling with the TV remote and muttering under her breath.

"Now, my dear Queenpin, I need you to pretend to die."

She looked up, her cat-eyes narrow slits. "Why should I? So you can be the boss?" She banged the remote against the arm of the sofa. "It's undignified to mock the dead."

"Don't consider it mocking the dead. Consider it a test drive. You'll get to see what your deluxe funeral at Neil Mansion looks like. And you'll get to see who shows up and what they say about you."

Her brow furrowed below her silver turban. "I'll be there?"

"Yes."

Sophia's wrinkly face puckered. "No way. I'm not getting in a coffin until I'm good and dead."

"Then you can be one of the mourners. An old friend from Sicily, perhaps? Think of it. You can find out what people *really* think of you. Maybe then you'll have enough information to choose your new heir."

The old woman scowled. "And what about the money for my *real* funeral?"

I smirked. "When that time comes, I don't think money is going to be a problem. Do you?"

"I see." Sophia's green eyes sparkled. "You're running a scam. Who's the mark?"

I chewed my bottom lip. "To be honest, I'm not sure. That's what I'm trying to find out. But if you don't cooperate, *you'll* be the patsy, for sure. I'm pretty sure someone's still actively trying to poison you."

Sophia shrugged. "Somebody's always trying to get me, one way or the other. I'm used to it."

"Aren't you tired of always having to look over your shoulder?"

Sophia sighed. "If it isn't me, it has to be *someone*. When I name an heir, that curse gets put on *their* head."

I shot the old woman a sympathetic smile. "Is that why you haven't named anyone?"

Sophia pursed her lips. "Look, Miss Know-It-All. I plan on going on living for as long as I can. So Edna and the others can live in relative peace. Capeesh?"

I shook my head. "Don't you get it, Sophia? There won't ever *be* peace until we find out who's willing to kill to be the new head of the family. I want to fake your death to see who comes out of the woodwork to claim your throne."

"No," Sophia grumbled. "I won't do it. If things go wrong, it could bring hell down on my girls."

I crossed my arms. "It *won't* go wrong. And you *will* do it."

Sophia smiled smugly. "You can't make me."

I pulled a fragile, yellowed slip of paper from my pocket. "You sure about that?"

Sophia glared at the paper in my hand. "What is that?"

"It's your original birth certificate. From Sicily."

Sophia's smug expression evaporated. "Where'd you get it?"

"That's not important right now. What *is*, is the fact that you're only ninety-six."

Sophia's droopy face fell an inch lower. She shook her head. "I *told* Harvey that would come back to haunt us one day. He made me lie about my age so we could get married. I was only sixteen." She stared at her gnarled hands. "He made me do a lot of things I didn't want to do."

"I had a feeling that might be the case. I wouldn't ask you to do this unless I really needed you to. For the Family."

Sophia glared at me. Her ancient, green eyes were an unreadable, shifting storm.

I thought about how she'd headed the Collard Green Cosa Nostra alone for the past thirty-five years. She'd buried her husband and her son. And she'd burned for over three decades with the belief that her only other child, Sammy had killed Saul and Harvey. Who would I have been in the face of all that?

I knelt down in front of Sophia. "With all due respect, your Queenpin, you are a living legend. It would be a travesty for you to lose your status as the oldest mafia leader in history."

Sophia scowled. "What are you talking about?"

"If your true age is made known, you'll become the laughing stock of the entire mafia. Do you want to be forever thought of as a demented old woman who doesn't even remember how old she is? And what will that do to the Family? We threw you a centennial party that was a complete sham. That alone will surely make us the joke of every other mafia family for decades to come."

Sophia sat there limp, but didn't say a word.

I touched her foot as a sign of respect. "You already scammed the Family, Sophia. This is your chance at redemption."

She glared at me. "And if I go along with your plan?"

"You and I keep this whole conversation between us, and the birth certificate disappears."

"Humph." Sophia wrapped her shawl a little tighter around her shoulders. "Omertà?"

"Omertà." I got up off my knees, kissed her hand, and offered her a tentative smile. "Act now, and I'll even throw in some new batteries for the TV remote."

Sophia's hard face cracked into a smirk. "Blackmail, Doreen? I didn't think you had it in you. Let me hear the rest of this plan of yours."

"Most certainly, your Queenpin. Come with me."

Chapter Thirty Five

My teeth were about to sink themselves into one of Morty's delicious, banana-pudding filled cannoli, when Kitty burst into the dining room.

Like kittens following a ball of string, Morty, Aunt Edna, Jackie, Sophia, and I all turned and stared at the resident potioneer. She was standing before us, huffing and puffing like an asthmatic puffer fish.

"You were right, Doreen!" Kitty gasped, her cheeks as pink as her shirt. "The sugar packets were laced with thallium!"

"Thallium?" I asked. I eyed the cannoli in my hand and set it back on my plate.

"Yes ... thallium." Kitty sucked in another lungful of air. "The poisoner's poison. Colorless ... odorless ... tasteless ... and bloody brilliant."

"How can that be?" Sophia asked, her cat eyes narrowed to slits. "I've been using those sugar packets for weeks."

Kitty gulped in a huge breath. "That's just it. The ones in the older baggie between the couch cushions only had trace amounts of thallium on them. But the new batch you and Jackie brought over earlier were covered with it."

"The rats upped the dosage," Morty said.

"Exactly." Kitty locked eyes with Sophia. "If you—or any of us—had touched them, we'd be on our way to the hospital right now. Or even the morgue."

"How did you know to test for thallium?" I asked.

"The symptoms you told me about," Kitty said. "Slow doses over time create symptoms similar to other illnesses. Hot feet. Hair loss. Pain in the joints."

"Got all three," Sophia said. She grimaced and pulled her shawl tighter. "Am I done for?"

"No." Kitty smiled softly at Sophia. "That's the good part. You're still breathing, so there's an antidote. Prussian Blue."

"You got any of that?" Aunt Edna asked.

"Of course." Kitty waved a small jar with a black lid. "What? You guys think I'm an amateur?"

"Hold on," Sophia said. "Has that stuff got any side effects?"

"Besides making you not die?" Kitty asked. "Well, constipation, maybe. And if you take enough, your sweat might turn blue."

Sophia shrugged. "Eh, nothing I haven't lived through before."

"Good. Sit tight. I'll run go make you a dose right now." Kitty took a step toward the kitchen, then turned back toward us and shook her head. "Sophia, you should be glad it wasn't oleander or rosary pea. If it had been, right now you'd be Snow White—minus the Prince Charming."

Sophia sighed. "Take it from me. Prince Charming isn't always what he's cracked up to be."

• • • •

"I DON'T GET IT," MORTY said while Kitty mixed up a dose of Prussian Blue for Sophia. "Why poison the sugar packets and not the coffee?"

"I thought about that myself," I said. "What it comes down to is proof."

Morty poured everyone another round of coffee. "Proof?"

I bit into a cannolo. "Yes," I mumbled through a mouthful. "There is no real ScarBux store. I looked it up. It doesn't exist. So the ScarBux sugar packets aren't available to anyone but the poisoner."

"So?" Jackie said. "I don't get it."

I licked banana cream from my lips. "Well, if their plan was to kill Sophia and take over as head of the Family, they'd need proof they were responsible. If they put the poison in the *coffee,* the evidence of where the thallium came from would be ambiguous."

"Who're Ambi and Gus?" Jackie asked.

I shook my head. "What I mean is, if the thallium was in the coffee, *anyone* could have said they put it there. But since it's on the ScarBux sugar packets, no one else but the poisoner would have them. They're indisputable proof."

Morty shook his head. "*Family* law is above the law. We'd have to let this jerk take over."

"Exactly," I said. "I think that's why they poisoned Sophia slowly. They hoped we wouldn't figure it out until it was too late. A swing and a miss with a big dose would've outed their game, and put a price on *their* head instead of Sophia's."

"Okay, say you're right," Aunt Edna said. "What do we do now?"

I smiled smugly. "My plan is to let them think they've won. We're going to stage Sophia's death."

"You're gonna make a play out of it?" Jackie asked.

I pressed my molars together. "No. We're going to hold a fake funeral and see who shows up with the sugar packets."

Morty rubbed his chin. "That could actually work."

I smiled. "Thanks."

"I guess that makes sense," Aunt Edna said. "But honestly, who would want to take over the CGCN? We're just a motley little crew now."

"I can think of two reasons right off the bat," I said. "One, to build it back up. And two, for the money."

Aunt Edna frowned. "Money? We ain't got no money."

"What about The Family Fund?" Jackie asked.

Morty grimaced. "I checked the bank balance last week. Believe me, it's not enough to kill for."

"Here she is," Kitty announced, helping Sophia back into the dining room. "Come on, Sophia. Show them! Please?"

"All right already," Sophia grumbled. She plopped down into a chair and stuck out her tongue. It was as blue as Papa Smurf's.

Jackie guffawed. Aunt Edna cackled. Morty snorted. And Kitty and I burst into belly laughs. Even the Queenpin herself couldn't help but snicker.

As we all fought to compose ourselves, Aunt Edna wiped tears of laughter from her eyes. "Well, we may be a broke-ass crew, but at least we can still laugh."

"Oh, we're not broke," I said. "Are we, Sophia?"

Sophia's snicker dried up. "What?"

I patted the yellowed paper tucked in my shirt pocket. The birth certificate wasn't the only secret Ma shared with me. "Do you want to tell them, or should I?"

Sophia sighed. "Fine. I'll tell them."

Chapter Thirty-Six

"So that's the plan," I said. "Everybody on board with it?"

All around the table, heads nodded.

"Then it's settled," I said. "Not a word of this to anyone. Only the other Family players we need to help pull this off. Can I get an Omertà?"

One by one, Morty, Aunt Edna, Jackie, Kitty, and, finally Sophia, repeated the mafia pledge of silence. "Omertà."

I nodded. "Good. Now, everybody get to work."

"I'll call Victor," Morty said. "And put some feelers out about Scar-Bux."

"I'll call Neil Mansion," Aunt Edna said. "I'll get the funeral arrangements set for noon tomorrow."

"Tomorrow?" Sophia grumbled. "Why so quick?"

"Hey, it's summer, remember?" Aunt Edna said. "You ain't getting any fresher. You're like Nosferatu. We gotta get you into the ground before you turn to dust. Besides, wouldn't you like to ruffle persnickety Neil Neil's feathers? He hates surprises."

Sophia grinned. "Yeah. Okay. So what do I do? Die of poisoning like a sick, old bird?"

"No," I said. "The fake coroner's report will say you died of natural causes."

"Why?" Kitty asked. "I thought the whole point was to get the poisoner to step up and take credit for their work."

"That's just it," I said. "Not being acknowledged should enrage the poisoner. Tell me. Do you know a man alive who doesn't expect a gold star for every little thing he does?"

"You make a good point," Aunt Edna said, shooting Morty some side-eye.

Morty grumbled. "Go ahead. Blame the men again."

"But what if it's not a man?" Jackie asked.

"It still works," Morty said. "Hell hath no fury like a woman scorned."

I grinned. "Touché."

"So, what about me?" Sophia repeated. "Do I just lay out in a coffin here like an expired slab of olive loaf?"

"No. We don't have time for a wake," I said. "It'll be a closed casket, too. But we *do* need you to lay low so you can't be spotted. That means you can't leave Edna's cottage until I give the word."

Sophia scowled. "Where am I gonna sleep?"

I glanced over at my aunt. "You can bunk with Aunt Edna."

"Nothing doing," Aunt Edna said. "This is *your* plan Dorey. Sophia bunks with *you*."

"But I don't have a TV in my room," I argued. "How's she gonna watch *Wheel of Fortune*?"

"Yeah?" Sophia said.

"No problem," Aunt Edna said. "I'll put my TV in your room, Dorey."

Sophia grunted. "Humph. Good to know I'm so deeply treasured."

"Now, don't get all riled up Sophia," Kitty said. "You need to rest." Kitty winked at me. "I'll get your room ready and watch over Sophia. I'll make sure she gets her antidotes on schedule. The Prussian Blue should work miracles in no time."

"Miracles, huh?" Jackie said. "Like raising Lavoris from the dead."

"*Lazarus*," Aunt Edna said. "Lavoris is a mouthwash."

"What?" Jackie frowned. "You telling me I've been drinking a capful of that stuff every morning for twenty years for *nothing*?"

Aunt Edna shot me a look. "Maybe *that's* what did it."

"Did what?" Jackie asked.

I stifled a smirk and slapped on a serious face. "Jackie, you're vital to this operation."

She cocked her head. "I am?"

"Yes. You're holding the lynch pin."

Confusion lined Jackie's narrow brow. "Uh ... I don't think I got one of those."

Aunt Edna and I exchanged glances.

I took Jackie by the hand. "What I *mean* is, it's your job to get the word out that the Queenpin suddenly dropped dead this morning. Right after drinking a cup of coffee."

"Oh." Jackie beamed at Sophia. "It would be my pleasure."

Sophia frowned, shook her head, then aimed her sour gaze at me. "What about *you*, Miss Bossy Pants. What are *you* gonna do?"

I grimaced. "Believe me, I saved the worst job for myself."

My plan to out Sophia's poisoner was flawless—except for one huge fly in the ointment.

Brady.

Somehow, I had to convince him I wasn't a rage-drunk, a vengeful vandalizing jerk, and a homicidal maniac.

No biggie.

Chapter Thirty-Seven

I checked my look in the mirror. Following Kitty's advice, I'd donned a pink blouse she'd lent me.

According to Kitty, the shirt wasn't just pink. It was "drunk-tank pink." The exact rosy hue law enforcement painted holding cells to calm inmates.

How Kitty knew this, I didn't ask. I only hoped it worked its charms on cops, too. Based on my last couple of conversations with Brady, I was going to need all the calming effects I could get.

After slipping into a pair of jeans and some pink kitten heels, I said a prayer to St. Jude, patron saint of lost causes, and headed for the living room. Aunt Edna was perched in the good chair, perusing the Neil Mansion Funeral's casket brochure.

"Have you called them yet?" I asked.

"Getting ready to. Want to make sure they give Sophia the works, like she paid for."

"What does it matter?" I asked.

Aunt Edna's eyebrow ticked up. "Until Sophia's really dead, we've still got to live with her."

"Point taken."

Aunt Edna scowled and shook her head. "I can't believe Sophia was holding out on us. All these years I've been running that stupid lonely hearts scam because I thought we were low on cash. Meanwhile, there she was over there, sitting on a wad of cash."

"Well, like you once told me, you can't expect to know all the Family secrets all at once."

"If you're trying to get on my good side, it's not working," Aunt Edna said.

"Sorry. Hey, did you ever figure out where those flowers came from?"

"My guess? Probably the same place as the ScarBux sugar packets."

I pursed my lips. "You're probably right. Okay if I borrow the Kia?"

"Sure. Where you going all dressed up?"

"To see Brady. We need him for the plan."

"You think you can trust him?" she asked.

"I have to. You think you can trust Morty?"

Aunt Edna blew out a sigh. "I have to."

My brow furrowed. "You two used to be an item. What happened between Morty and you?"

"He thought I did something I didn't do."

"What?"

Aunt Edna frowned and shook her head. "He accused me of stepping out on him. I couldn't believe he would think I would do something so low."

"You couldn't convince him otherwise?"

"Why should I *have* to?" Aunt Edna snapped.

I winced. "So what happened?"

"You got eyes, don't you? It ruined things between us, Dorey."

"What did?"

"Pigheadedness."

"Oh." I chewed my bottom lip. "On whose part?"

Aunt Edna sighed. "On both of ours."

• • • •

I TOOK OFF TO MAKE amends with Brady. But I didn't get far. I'd no sooner driven The Toad a block from Palm Court Cottages when a siren sounded. Behind me, blue-and-red lights began flashing. I groaned.

I can't get busted now! How will the plan go on without me?

I watched through the rearview mirror as the cop climbed out of his cruiser.

It was Brady.

He marched toward me, his handsome face as hard and steely as that half-robot policeman in *RoboCop*.

I rolled down the window. My heart fluttered in my chest. It was do or die time. Literally.

"You're supposed to be under house arrest!" Brady barked as he reached my window.

I cringed and bit my lip. "I know."

Come on, drunk-tank pink! Do you thing!

"But you didn't say *which* house," I said, trying to sound both humble and like a damsel in distress.

"What are you talking about?" Brady growled.

Thanks a lot, stupid pink shirt.

I took a deep breath and just went for it. "Brady, you and I both know that if I don't do something to clear my name from the Eddie Houser suspect list, I could end up living in this car, on the lam. So, technically, the Kia could be considered my house, right?"

Brady shook his head. "Doreen, sometimes your logic ... *defies logic.* You know I can't just let you break the law."

"I'm not asking you to."

"Then what are you asking?"

"For a chance to explain. Give me ten minutes and I'll give you the truth."

"About what?"

"About everything."

Chapter Thirty-Eight

"First off, I want to apologize about your truck," I said, smiling tentatively at Brady from the passenger seat of his police cruiser. "I was angry that you didn't take me seriously about Humpty Bogart. And ..." I winced. "I'd been drinking."

"Yes, you had. Polished off almost a whole bottle of wine by yourself."

I pursed my lips. "I'm trying to apologize, here."

Brady's hard face softened. "Right. Sorry."

"Anyway, when you blew me off by laughing at my suggestion, I kind of ... *lost it.* I'm sorry that in my anger I accidently scratched your truck."

"Accidentally?" Brady said. "*That's* what you call it when you scratch the word PIG into the side of someone's truck?"

My mouth fell open. "What? I didn't do that! I only kicked your bumper."

I think.

"What? You didn't scratch the word PIG into my truck's passenger door panel?"

I shook my head. "No! How could I? When would I have had the opportunity?"

Brady chewed on that for a moment. "So you really didn't—"

"No. I swear!"

Brady frowned. "If you didn't, who did?"

"How should I know? *You're* the cop. Shouldn't you ..." I stopped mid-sentence. "Wait a minute. It could've been the guy I saw waving a knife at me while you paid the check."

"What?" Brady practically squealed. "You saw a guy with a knife and you didn't bother to mention it?"

I bit my bottom lip. "Well, I *think* it was a guy. And it *could've* been a knife. I couldn't see their face. They were wearing a hoodie and standing by your truck."

"And you're just telling me this now?"

My shoulders stiffened. "Yes. It's the first time you've given me a chance to explain anything without cutting me off first."

Brady sighed. "Fair enough."

I reached over and touched his hand. "Sorry about your truck."

He nodded. "Sorry about you getting tangled up in another homicide investigation."

"I didn't do *that*, either."

We both smiled and shook our heads. Then, as if on cue, we simultaneously laughed.

"How do you keep getting into these messes?" Brady asked.

I shook my head again. "I dunno. Just lucky, I guess."

"Me, too." Brady's brow furrowed. "Why would some random person scratch the word PIG on my truck? How would they even know I'm a cop?"

My right eyebrow rose an inch. "Are you kidding? Everything about you screams cop, Brady."

"It does not."

"Cop haircut. Cop body language. Cop attitude."

"Oh, really? How about this?" Brady leaned across the seat and kissed me hard on the mouth. "Do I *kiss* like a cop, too?"

I smirked. "I can't say. You're my first policeman. But I *can* say this. You kiss better than Tad Longmire. And way better than the guy who works the drive-thru at the In-N-Out Burger in LA."

Brady shot me a sideways smile. "Nice to know I'm not at the bottom of your list, Diller."

I grinned and leaned in to kiss him again. But as I did, the playful sparkle in Brady's eyes disappeared.

"Now, tell me about that pool of human blood McNulty found on the curb outside your apartment, Diller. How did you know it was Eddie Houser's?"

Chapter Thirty-Nine

Brady shook his head and took a slurp of his Dairy Hog milkshake. "And here I was, thinking they were just a bunch of harmless little old ladies."

"They *are*, Brady." I set down my chili dog. "They didn't *kill* Eddie. They just found him and called somebody to remove his body. They only did it to protect me."

"Protect you from what?"

I shot him a look. "Myself. Okay? You know my track record for this type of thing. I'm the queen of self-incrimination."

Brady nodded. "Okay. But you said they found Houser inside a car."

"Yes. A Nissan Cube the color of Kermit's keister."

"What happened to the car?"

"They had it ... uh ... removed."

"I see. Along with the murder weapon?"

"No, we took that to—"

"Hold on," Brady said, showing me his palm. "We?" He shook his head. "Doreen, this is *so* not good. Perhaps I should remind you that you have the right to remain silent?"

I locked eyes with Brady. "I appreciate that. But Brady, I don't have anything to hide. Somebody's trying to *frame* me. They took the baseball bat out of the Kia, killed Eddie with it, then put it back in Aunt Edna's car to make it look like I did it."

"The killer put the bat *back* in the ..." Brady's eyes bore into mine. "Let me get this straight. You're telling me someone drove Houser to your apartment and he just sat there patiently in the Nissan while they got out, stole the bat from your car, then came back and bludgeoned him to death right in front of your place? And then the killer simply put the baseball bat back in your car and went on his merry way?"

I winced. "Well, not exactly."

Brady blew out a breath. "Thank you."

I stared intently into Brady's eyes. "I think Eddie drove himself to my place and was ambushed."

Brady's brow furrowed. "What exactly would Houser be doing at your place, anyway?"

"He wanted to give me a discount on the Nissan. As payment, instead of the profit-sharing scheme I'd originally agreed to."

"Wait a minute. You talked to Houser before he was murdered?"

"No. All that stuff was spelled out in the contract lying next to his body."

Brady pinched the bridge of his nose. "And where is this contract now?"

I winced. "Uh ... I don't know."

"Putting that aside for the moment, do you have any idea who would want to kill Houser?"

"I'd say pretty much anyone who ever met him. He was a pig."

Brady's face puckered. "As in P-I-G?"

I grimaced. "Unfortunate use of the descriptive."

"Right," Brady said. "We need to narrow the suspects down from the entire human population. Do you have any idea who would want to kill Houser and frame *you* for it?"

I thought about it for a moment. "No. I mean, generally, I'm a nice person."

Brady laughed. "This isn't not a personality contest, Diller. Innocent people get framed all the time. That's why we call it getting framed. So, do you know anyone who might have it out for you?"

"Maybe Humpty Bogart? I mean, *Humphrey Bogaratelli*? Or someone I pissed off by doing that sexist commercial for Eddie's car lot? Or wait ... maybe whoever scratched PIG into your car?"

Brady frowned. "Would any of them have access to the Kia?"

"Probably. Jackie drives it a lot. She never locks the doors."

Brady blew out a breath. "So anyone could have taken the bat out of your car."

I nodded. "Yeah. Pretty much."

"Doreen, answer me this, would you?"

"Sure." I raised the hotdog to my mouth. "What?"

"What were you doing with a baseball bat in your car in the first place?"

"Oh. Jackie gave it to me. For good luck."

"Yeah? How's that working out for you?"

I shrugged. "I don't know yet."

"Argh! Doreen, why are you so ... so ..."

"Unlucky?" I asked.

Brady shook his head.

I raised the hotdog to my mouth. "Ridiculous?"

"Yes, but no."

I took a bite of hotdog. Mustard squirted onto my shirt. "Disaster prone?"

"No." Brady pursed his lips. "The word I'm searching for is ... irresistible."

My mouth full of hotdog fell open. "Are you serious?"

Brady shook his head softly. "Unfortunately, yes. Against all my better judgement, I can't stop thinking about you."

"Wait a minute." I swallowed and wiped my mouth with a paper napkin. "You're not worried I'm a killer?"

"No."

My heart skipped a beat—in a good way. "But what about the bloody thumbprints on the jeans you stole out of my washing machine?"

"*Confiscated*," Brady corrected. "And no, I'm not worried about them. It turns out, the prints were actually ketchup with a little cornmeal and old fryer grease mixed in."

"Ketchup from a corndog. *Told* you."

"Yes, you did."

I grinned and took a savage, celebratory bite from my hotdog.

Brady shook his head. "Only you, Doreen. Only you."

• • • •

AFTER A MAKE-OUT SESSION in Brady's squad car in an alley behind the Dairy Hog, I filled Brady in on my plan to fake Sophia's death and entrap the person poisoning her.

"Who knows?" I said between lip-locks with the handsome cop. "Maybe we'll catch Eddie's killer in the process."

Brady stopped kissing me. "You think they're related?"

I shrugged. "Maybe. Aunt Edna told me Humpty and Eddie might've been working in cahoots to steal from the Family Fund. Maybe their partnership went south."

"Louisville Slugger south." Brady said. "It makes sense."

"Hey, now that we've kissed and made up, I just wanted to say that I can see how you thought the name Humpty Bogart was a joke. But believe me, if my hunch about him is right, he's definitely no one to be taken lightly. That's why I need your help with my plan."

Brady pursed his swollen lips. "Like I told you before, I can't do anything illegal to help you, Doreen. I'd lose my job. *And* it's against my principles."

"I'm not asking you to do anything you haven't done for my aunt and her friends before. Just hang around the apartments in plain clothes tomorrow. Keep an eye out on the property while we're at the funeral."

"Do you think the women are in danger?"

"No, I don't think so. Whoever was trying to do Sophia in thinks that mission's been accomplished."

"Then why do you want me to watch the place?"

"Because if my scheme goes according to plan, someone's going to try and break into Sophia's cottage during her funeral service and make off with the Family Fund. And when they do, I'll need you to be there to aid in the apprehension."

"Aid in the apprehension?" Brady frowned. "Does that mean you don't plan on being at the apartments?"

I chewed my lip. "I haven't decided yet."

"Geez, Diller. This plan of yours seems to have a few holes in it."

I nodded. "Yeah, but you can't account for every little thing, now can you?"

Brady sighed. "I suppose not. Anything else you need me to do?"

I smiled and kissed Brady. "Well, since you asked, in about a half an hour, we're going to be carrying Sophia out in a body bag. Your police cruiser at the scene would add a nice touch of authenticity."

Brady shook his head. "I had a feeling I was going to regret this."

"Which part?"

Brady smirked. "I haven't decided yet."

Chapter Forty

When we pulled up to Palm Court Cottages in Brady's police cruiser, operation "Sophia the Stiff" was already well under-way.

A black hearse was parked where the Kia normally stood. Two men were huffing and puffing down the garden path, hauling a black body bag toward the street.

I recognized the meaty, ex-prize-fighter face of one of the men. It was Morty. The tall and lanky one had to be Victor the Vulture. After all, he was the one who made bodies disappear. Looking like the love child of Lurch and Elvira, Victor seemed born for the job.

Trailing behind the men were Kitty, Aunt Edna, and Jackie. Each was putting on an academy award performance worthy of Shirley Mc-Clain in *Terms of Endearment.*

I laughed out loud. Jackie heard me. She looked up and beamed a Poligrip smile, followed by a thumb's up.

Brady shook his head. "I'm assuming Sophia isn't really in that body bag?"

I smirked. "I thought you said you wanted to know as little about this as possible."

"Right. But if her life is at stake—"

"She's not in the bag."

"What is?"

"Believe me, you really don't want to know."

• • • •

I WAS SITTING ON AUNT Edna's green velvet couch compliment-ing Jackie, Kitty and Aunt Edna on their acting skills when Morty came through the front door.

"The 'body of evidence' is in transit," he said, then smiled at me. "Nice touch having Brady's cruiser park outside."

"Thanks." I smiled at the four elderly mobsters. "Phase one of Sophia the Stiff is officially complete. But Morty, I thought you were going with Victor."

"I was. But I thought I'd better stick around. While he and I were loading the hearse, I spotted a couple of suspicious vehicles cruising around."

"Wow," Kitty said. "Word of Sophia's demise has already hit the streets."

I shot Jackie a thumb's up. "Good work."

She grinned. "I do what I can."

"I do, too," Aunt Edna said, somewhat grumpily. "In case anyone's interested, the funeral's all set for noon tomorrow." She smiled smugly. "Neil Neil wasn't too keen on the idea, but after promising to book my own funeral if he pulled off this one for Sophia, he changed his tune pretty quick."

"Excellent," I said.

Aunt Edna shot a look at Sophia. "I ordered the works for myself."

Sophia scowled beneath her silver turban. "I hope you didn't skimp on the hor d'oeuvres for tomorrow. I don't want people thinking I went cheap."

"I got it all taken care of," Morty said. "You'll have a shrimp tower as tall as a mountain, and a spread that could make the cover of *Southern Living.*"

Sophia smiled smugly and rubbed her gnarled hands together. "I can't wait to see the looks on their faces."

"You're gonna be there?" Jackie asked. "I thought you were gonna be dead."

"She is," I said. "But Sophia's coming as her old friend visiting from Sicily. She'll wear a black veil to cover her face."

"Oh." Jackie cocked her head. "What's your friend's name?"

Sophia's face puckered. "Brunhilda. Okay?"

"Huh," Jackie said. "I thought she was from Sicily, not Austria."

Sophia shook her head and looked at me. "I still can't decide if that's her personality, or some kind of disorder."

"Moving on," I blurted. "With the transfer done, we need to keep Sophia out of sight and hope the funeral goes off without a hitch. Jackie, who do you think will show up?"

Jackie shrugged. "Everybody. People have been waiting a hundred years for Sophia to croak."

I hazarded a quick glance at Sophia. She looked as if her turban were about to explode.

"Uh ... Morty!" I said. "I was wondering if that other bag man who works with Humpty might show his face tomorrow."

"Vinny Zamboni?" Morty said. "Not likely. Victor told me he picked up Vinny's body three days ago. It's still on ice waiting on an autopsy."

"That's a crying shame," Jackie said.

"Speaking of crying," Sophia said, eying us with aggravation. "I hope you gals put on as big a waterworks show as you did today when I really *do* kick the bucket."

"Of course we will," Kitty said.

"'Cause I'll still be watching," Sophia said. "You can count on it." The old woman straightened in her seat and tugged on her shawl. "So, now on to more important matters. What's for lunch?"

Chapter Forty-One

I was at the Texaco when it happened.

The ever-ravenous Sophia had demanded fried chicken and collard greens for lunch. The only place in town that met Aunt Edna's standards was a food truck in the parking lot of the Texaco on Ninth Street.

So while the others dug through their closets assembling outfits for the funeral tomorrow, I volunteered to pick up the fried chicken—on stern orders from my aunt not to get suckered into buying the corn on the cob.

I'd just paid for our massive lunch order and was sinking my teeth into a mushy, tasteless ear of over-boiled corn when someone snuck up behind me and beaned me over the head.

"Ow!" I yelled, then dropped the corn and whirled around. Glaring at me from behind inch-thick, horn-rimmed glasses was a short, elderly woman somewhere between the ages of 70 and 800.

"Murderer!" she hissed, waving an empty Coke bottle in the air like a club.

I rubbed the rising knot on the back of my head. "Geez, lady. I didn't kill Tad Longmire. It was *pretend*. It was only a show on TV!"

"What are you talking about?" the old woman growled. "I'm talking about the viral video on TakTok. Thanks to you, I missed out on Crazy Eddie's deal of a lifetime on a Dodge Durango!"

"What?"

The old woman in a house dress and orthopedic shoes took another swing at me. I took a step toward the Kia. She took a step to block my way.

"Where do you think you're going?" she hissed.

Geez. That must've been one great discount on that Durango.

My path to the Kia currently inaccessible, I tightened by grip on the sacks of fried chicken and did the only thing I could think of. I ran like an idiot to the side of the Texaco and lock myself in the washroom.

For an eternity lasting about five minutes, I tried not to touch anything or breathe in the smelly air. Suddenly, a knock sounded on the door.

"Occupied," I yelled.

"I gotta pee!" a woman's muffled voice yelled back. "Are you coming out anytime in the next century?"

I grimaced. "Is there an old lady out their wielding a Coke bottle?"

"What?"

"I said, is there an old lady out their wielding a Coke bottle?"

"Uh ... no. Why?"

I flung open the restroom door and sucked in a deep breath. "Thanks. It's all yours," I said to the woman. Then I realized it was Shirley Saurwein.

I looked up at the heavens. "Seriously?"

"Seriously what?"

My gaze returned to the bleach-blonde bane of my existence. "What are you doing here?"

She glanced at the paper sacks in my hand. "Same as you. They've got the best chicken in town. You eating for eight now? Don't tell me you're gonna be the next octamom."

"Ha ha." I rubbed the knot on my head and began walking past her. "And just for the record, I had nothing to do with how that place smells."

"Yeah," she cracked. "I bet you say that to *all* the ladies."

I took another step. Suddenly, two-and-two came together in my head. I whirled back around. "Wait a minute. Was it you who released that video of me slashing Eddie Houser's neck with that stupid rubber knife?"

Saurwein grinned and waggled her eyebrows. "Oh. So you've seen my work."

I gritted my teeth. "Yes."

"Pretty good, eh? It's up to 237,000 views!" Saurwein squealed in delight. She flipped through her cellphone and shoved the screen in my face. "Look. It even beat out the alligator riding an ATV."

"Geez, Saurwein!" I hissed. "Don't you realize how harmful those videos can be? Thanks to the new '*digital age*,' people can't tell the difference between reality and entertainment anymore."

"I know!" She wagged her eyebrows. "And *I'm* cashing in on it!"

I glared at her. "Unbelievable!"

"It sure is!" Saurwein waved her phone at me. "You probably don't know this, Diller, but it's a biological fact that the human brain can't tell the difference between real events and pixels on an electronic screen. The poor saps can't help themselves!"

I didn't have a gun, so I shot the sketchy reporter a sneer instead. "Believe me, Saurwein, that's no consolation to the victims when they get knocked in the head by an old lady armed with a Coke bottle."

"Oh, is *that* what this is all about?" Saurwein shrugged and cracked her gum.

I blew out a breath. "I guess I should thank you for not printing a picture of me slashing Eddie on the cover of today's *Beach Gazette*."

Saurwein frowned. "Don't thank me. That was my game plan. You, slitting Eddie's throat, right next to the article about how the guy suddenly disappeared. But my stupid editor started yammering some nonsense about slander and yellow journalism, so your pic didn't make the cut. Plus, I needed to let the heat die down."

"The heat?"

"My editor's been getting a few angry calls from some disgruntled women."

"Gee, I wonder why?" I shook my head. "You know, Saurwein, we women should work *together*, not tear each other apart."

"Oh. Sorry, Diller. I didn't realize you're a woman." Saurwein winked at me. "Here's a tip on the house. Whatever you're using to get rid of your moustache? It ain't working."

"Arrgh!" I growled. "Why do you hate me?"

Saurwein shot me a pair of pouty lips. "Aww. I don't hate you, Diller. But when it comes to local tabloid news, you're top of the food chain right now."

"How do I get off your food chain?"

"Three ways. Die. Leave town. Or pray some other poor sap even more pathetic than you crawls out from under a rock."

An evil grin curled my lips. "What if I could give you a scoop? Something way tastier than me?"

Saurwein's right eyebrow crooked. "I'm listening."

Chapter Forty-Two

Good thing I put swearing in the car alone in the same category as the calories in broken cookies. Neither counted. I'd just made a pact with a devil in red lipstick. I only hoped it didn't come back to haunt me.

As I slammed on the brakes and cursed out a red traffic light, my cellphone rang. It was Brady. My heart fluttered.

"Hey," I said, trying to sound casual.

"Hey, yourself. Just calling to say hi, and to give you a heads up."

"Heads up?"

"An escaped prisoner was spotted in the downtown St. Pete area about an hour ago. I thought you should know."

"Why? Should I interview them as a potential cellmate?"

"No. I told you, I believe you. You didn't kill Eddie."

"Then why—"

"The convict's name is Marco Telleroni. Aka, *Monkey-Face Mongo*. It turns out he's real."

"I know. My aunt told me. He's one of her ... uh ..."

Crap!

"Diller!" Brady gasped. "Is this guy your aunt's prison pen pal?"

I cringed. "Yes. Does it say in his file why they called him Monkey-Face Mongo?"

"No need to. The mugshot says it all."

I laughed.

"This isn't a joke, Doreen. They guy was serving life for murder. You should talk to your aunt. Make sure she's not being swindled by this conman."

"Maybe she's the one swindling *him*," I said. "You ever think about that?"

"Either way, it would be wrong."

"I say if Aunt Edna can con guys like these back, they had it coming."

"*Guys* like these? How many are there?"

I cringed again.

Double crap!

"I don't have an exact count ..."

"Doreen, no one deserves to be preyed upon."

"Yeah? Well men like that take advantage of women all the time."

"An eye for an eye leaves us all blind and toothless."

I scowled. "Who died and appointed you the new Yoda?"

I heard Brady blow out a breath. "I'm just worried about you and the other ladies, that's all."

The tone in his voice made *me* worry, too. "Brady, my aunt and her friends have been taking care of themselves for longer than we've been alive."

"That's my point, Doreen. They're old. They're not as invincible as they may think they once were."

"I get it," I said. "I promise I'll talk to Aunt Edna when I get home."

"Where are you?"

"I just left the chicken place at the Texaco."

"Oh. Nice. They have the best chicken in town. I may stop by there myself."

"If you do, here's a heads up for *you*. Don't order the corn on the cob."

"Everybody knows that."

"And one other thing. Watch out for old ladies with Coke bottles."

"What?"

"Don't ask." The red light turned green. "I gotta go."

• • • •

AFTER STUFFING OURSELVES with fried chicken and collard greens, I joined Aunt Edna in the kitchen for a TUMS chaser.

As we both crunched on a couple of chalky tablets, we washed up the dishes and talked about Mongo, Morty, and life's other relationship mysteries.

"Could Mongo have sent the flowers?" I asked, rinsing a plate in the sink. "Do you think he could've found out where we live?"

Aunt Edna's brow furrowed. "Mongo's got connections. He could find out anything he wanted to." She snatched the plate from me and began drying it with a dish towel. "Do me a favor, Dorey. Don't say anything to the other women about it."

"Why not?"

"It might ... uh ... scare them."

"More the reason they should know." I scrubbed the grease from another plate. "Maybe it would be good for Morty to stay with us tonight. To have some muscle around. You know, as reinforcement."

"He can't." Aunt Edna placed the dried plate in the cupboard atop the others. "Morty's pulling an all-nighter to get the catering for the funeral done."

I shot her a soft smile. "Sounds like he really cares."

She shrugged. "He's been good to us."

"Then why not rekindle the flame?" I handed her the final plate to dry. "Why not go out with Morty again?"

She shook her head. "It's too late. I've let myself go. Look at me. I've gained twenty pounds since Morty and I last went out."

"Is that *all*?" Jackie asked, peeking around the corner.

Aunt Edna shot her nosy sidekick some serious side eye. "Too bad I ain't like Jackie here, who has the amazing butt."

Jackie stepped into the kitchen and twisted around to get a gander at her backside. "I do?"

"Yeah," Aunt Edna said. "Every time you walk away, I can't help but think, 'What an ass.'"

Jackie beamed. "Thanks, Edna."

• • • •

AFTER AUNT EDNA CHASED Jackie out of her apartment with her rolling pin, the two of us went and sat in the living room to finish our chat while Sophia was in the restroom.

"There's more to Mongo than you're letting on, isn't there?" I asked, sitting down on the sofa.

Aunt Edna grimaced from her perch in the Barcalounger. "He used to be sweet on me."

"What happened?"

Her eyebrow crooked upward. "Have you seen his face?"

"Uh ... no."

"Let me put it this way. You ever watch *BJ and the Bear*?"

"The show with the truck driver and the chimpanzee?"

"Yeah. Well, Mongo looks like the one who ain't driving."

"Looks aren't everything," I said.

"No, they ain't. But you gotta draw the line somewhere. Mine is you gotta look like a member of the human race."

I laughed.

"See?" Aunt Edna said, scowling. "That's what I'm afraid of. If the other women knew Mongo was sweet on me, I'd never live it down."

I snickered. "I get it. Mum's the word."

"Thanks. You know, Dorey, when I was younger, I always hoped something good would happen to me. Now I just hope whatever crappy thing happens will at least be amusing."

"But Brady told me Mongo was no laughing matter."

My aunt's eyes doubled in size. "You told him about us?"

"Only that he was one of your lonely-hearts scam guys."

"You told him I was running a lonely-hearts scam!"

I winced. "Not exactly. He thinks you're the *victim* of the scam, not the one running it."

Aunt Edna shook her head. "I'm not so sure which is worse."

"If Mongo does find you, what do you think he'll do?"

"I dunno. But right now, we've both got other things to worry about."

I sighed. "You're right. I think I'll call Brady and ask him to keep an eye on the place overnight."

"Oh. I was talking about dinner. With all this commotion, I haven't had time to get to the grocery store."

Chapter Forty-Three

"What is this? A hamster?" Sophia complained as Aunt Edna set her dinner in front of her.

"It's quail," Aunt Edna said. "They were on sale. I bought them before I found out you were actually Granny Warbucks."

"Humph," Sophia grumbled. "There isn't enough meat on this thing to keep a cockroach alive."

"At least it's not a rat," Kitty said, removing a pink visor from her head. "Did you know Queen Elizabeth was once served a gibnut while she was in Belize?"

"A gibbon?" Jackie asked.

"No," Kitty said. "A *gibnut*. It's a member of the rodent family."

My upper lip snarled. "Well, let's hope we catch the rodent who's been infesting *our* Family tomorrow."

Kitty smirked coyly. "Speaking of rats. Edna, have you heard anything more about Mongo?"

Aunt Edna choked on a sip of iced tea. "No. Thank heavens. Listen. I've learned my lesson. No more lonely hearts clubs for me. Real *or* fake."

"What about Morty?" Kitty asked. "There's still a chance there, isn't there?"

"Yeah," Jackie said. "I think Morty's still got the hots for you, Edna."

"No he ain't." Aunt Edna scowled. "That spark went out years ago. Sophia's right. When you get old, *food's* the only real pleasure you got left."

"Of course I'm right," Sophia said, stabbing her fork at the tiny bird carcass on her plate. "But now I'm beginning to wonder about *that*, too."

"Aww, come on, Aunt Edna," I said, nudging her. "Morty seems like a nice guy to me."

Aunt Edna blew out a breath. "I dunno. The whole idea of dating again is ... *horrifying*. I think I'd rather go to jail."

"I can't argue with you," Kitty said. "I don't think there's any bigger blow to a woman's ego than being dumped by an old geezer whose portrait should be hanging in the comb-over hall of fame."

Jackie laughed. "I remember that guy. Gary, right?"

Kitty shook her head. "Yes."

"What about that guy Blane?" Jackie asked. "He seemed okay. Or was that just the toupee talking?"

Kitty rolled her eyes. "Blane *did* put some good money into his bridgework. I'd give him that. But solid dentistry isn't enough to build a relationship on."

"Jackie, whatever happened to Walter?" Aunt Edna asked. "He had a kind of infectious smile."

"Turned out to be herpes," Jackie said. "Nope. I say the best man to date is the pizza delivery guy."

I nearly dropped my fork. "What? Why?"

Jackie shrugged. "Because you know right off the bat he's got a car, a job, and a pizza."

Sophia shook her head. "Listen to you all! You youngsters still have it made. At my age, the best a woman can hope for is a little hair on the guy's head and a mouth that doesn't look like it's harboring some kind of disease."

I elbowed Aunt Edna. "Morty's sounding pretty good about now, eh?"

She sighed. "I dunno. I think he's more into young chicks like you, Dorey."

"If he is, he's too late," Jackie said. "Dorey's sweet on Brady."

"I am not!"

Jackie wagged her eyebrows. "Then why was you two doing the mush-mouth pretzel in his squad car this morning?"

My mouth fell open. All around the dining table, every face turned and smirked at me.

I cringed. "You saw that, huh?"

"Me and everybody else who passed you two on the sidewalk. Including Benny here." Jackie leaned down and patted the ancient pug lying in wait for table scraps. "And you wanna know something?"

I grimaced. "Not really."

"Benny here didn't get a single whiff of deadbeat, did you, girl?"

"Huh," I grunted. "Well, I guess that's something."

"So, are you and Brady an item?" Kitty asked.

I shrugged. "I don't know yet."

Sophia jabbed her fork in my direction. "Does he play the guitar?"

I cocked my head. "I don't know. Why?"

Sophia's green eyes locked on mine. "I'm always leery of anything with strings attached."

"Me, too," Jackie said. "I can't stand raw celery."

Aunt Edna threw her hands in the air. "*Food*, I'm telling you! It's all we've got left!" She shook her head. "What's a person to do when eating becomes the best thing they got going in their life?"

"Easy," Jackie said. "Get a better life."

• • • •

AFTER DINNER, SOPHIA, Aunt Edna, and I retired to the living room to watch TV. After a riveting round of *Wheel of Fortune*, Sophia announced she was ready for bed.

My bed.

With her bunking in my room, I'd been relegated to the couch. I suppose that's why I found it so disconcerting when the old Queenpin farted into the cushion where my head would soon lie.

"Hey, look," Aunt Edna said, flipping through the *TV Guide*. It says here your show's on tonight, Dorey."

"What show?" I asked.

"*Beer & Loathing.*"

"Gee. I can't wait," I groaned as I helped Sophia to her feet.

Aunt Edna clicked the remote to Channel 22. I watched warily as the opening scene of *Beer & Loathing* came on the screen. Playing serial killer Doreen Killigan had been the highlight of my pathetic acting career. Still, even *I* wasn't that keen on watching it again.

I took Sophia by the arm. "Come on, off to bed."

Suddenly, the show was interrupted by breaking news.

"Wait. What's that about?" Sophia asked.

We stood and stared at the TV set as a couple of standard-issue news anchors came on the screen.

"The police have issued a be-on-the-lookout warning for escaped fugitive, Marco Telleroni," the woman anchor said. "He was serving a life term for murder, and is considered armed and dangerous."

A picture of Telleroni's mugshot flashed full screen, accompanied by the anchorman's voiceover. He warned viewers, "If you see this fugitive, please report any and all information immediately to the local authorities."

"Ha!" Sophia cackled. "Who are we supposed to call? The police or a zookeeper?"

Chapter Forty-Four

I grumbled and turned over on the velveteen couch.

Go to sleep, Doreen!

Between smelling the ghosts of Sophia's farts and imagining Mongo's monkey face peeking in the windows, I was having a hard time nodding off.

But when someone tapped lightly on the front door, I knew I wasn't just making it up.

My heart began thumping in my throat. I bolted upright and scrambled for a weapon. Aunt Edna's figurine of St. Christopher would have to do. Holding it in my fist like a knife, I tiptoed to the front door and peeked through the peephole.

I nearly fainted with relief. It was Brady.

I cracked opened the door to find the handsome cop wearing dark jeans and a black T-shirt. His hair was slicked back like The Fonz on *Happy Days*.

"What are you doing here?" I whispered.

He glanced at the statuette in my hand. "Answering your prayers, apparently."

"What?" I glanced down at poor St. Christopher. "Ha ha."

Brady grinned. "You asked me to come over, remember? So as soon as I got off shift, I got a shower and headed over."

"Oh. Right."

His dark eyes twinkled playfully. "I figured I could keep an eye on the place just as well from the inside as the outside, don't you think?"

I chewed my bottom lip. "I dunno. What if Mongo shows up?"

Brady smirked. "And what? Catches us monkeying around?"

I laughed. "Shut up and kiss me."

He grinned. "I thought you'd never ask."

I WOKE UP AT THE CRACK of dawn. Oddly, I thought I smelled bacon frying.

Dang. Maybe it's true. Food really is *one of the last pleasures in life.*

But it wasn't *the* last one. Not for *me*, anyway. I smiled coyly, remembering last night.

Then I *totally freaked*, remembering last night. Brady had spent the night here with me!

I heard a toilet flush. I sat up on one elbow and spotted Brady's shoes tucked beside the old Barcalounger.

Holy crap! Brady's still here!

I scrambled off the couch and met him in the hallway. He had on his jeans, but no T-shirt. Those washboard abs looked strikingly familiar ...

"Brady!" I whispered, tugging him by the arm. "You have to get out of here! Quick!"

He grinned. "Can I at least get my shirt back first?"

I looked down. I was wearing it. "Double crap."

I heard the coffee machine begin to perk. Before I could say a word, Aunt Edna peeked around the corner.

"So, is lover boy staying for breakfast?" she asked. "I'm making my famous egg-noodle quiche."

My face flamed as red as a thousand suns.

Brady laughed. "Sure, Mrs. Barker. I'd love to stay."

Aunt Edna smiled. "Good. I'll set another place at the table."

As my aunt disappeared back into the kitchen, Brady pulled me to him and kissed me on the nose.

"Hey, Diller. You ever get the feeling we're like Hansel and Gretel, only the house is made of linguini?"

"Yeah."

All. The. Time.

••••

AS I SAT AT THE BREAKFAST table with Brady and my Italian mob family, I felt like Cher in *Moonstruck*. Here we all were, biding our time, waiting for whatever fate would soon befall us.

Mercifully, the conversation had kept to casual morning greetings—along with a few smirks and furtive, darting eyes. As for the Queenpin, Sophia seemed oblivious to the handsome newcomer sitting at the table. Her nose was buried in the Sunday edition of the *Tampa Bay Times*.

"Nothing!" she hissed, then tossed the crumpled newspaper aside.

"What are you talking about?" Aunt Edna asked.

"I didn't make the front page," Sophia grumbled. "Not even the obits."

Aunt Edna sat her coffee cup down. "That's because I didn't post one."

Sophia's cat eyes narrowed. "Why not?"

Aunt Edna shot her a look. "Because you're not *really dead*!"

"Humph." The Queenpin's glare switched over to me. "Where's my ScarBux?"

Seriously?

"Sorry," I said. "The guy didn't show up this morning." Just as I'd expected.

"Why not?" Sophia grumbled.

I shrugged. "Probably because he thinks you're dead."

Sophia chewed on that a moment, then tugged the ends of her shawl together and grumbled, "Can't depend on anybody nowadays."

Brady squeezed my hand under the table and whispered, "Is she always this feisty?"

I smirked. "Only when she's conscious."

"All right, everybody, breakfast is a wrap," Aunt Edna announced. She stood and began gathering up empty plates. "It's time to get going. We've got a big day ahead."

"That's right," Jackie said. "Especially you, Sophia. This is the day you drop dead."

Sophia glared at Jackie. "If only I could say the same about you, Jackie, I could die a happy woman."

Jackie grinned. "Well, ain't that nice."

Chapter Forty-Five

"Double up on the gauze," I said to Kitty. "We don't want anyone recognizing her."

"Got it." Kitty added another layer of netting on Sophia's black veil. "How's this?"

"Geez," Sophia grumbled, waving a hand in front of her face. "I can hardly see through this thing. I might walk into a wall or something."

"You won't," Kitty said. "One of us will be by your side at all times, to make sure you're safe." Kitty winked at me and whispered, "And to make sure she doesn't let the cat out of the bag."

"I'm only blind, not deaf," Sophia said. "And it's *Jackie* you've got to worry about spilling the beans. Not *me*."

"Yes, Brunhilda," Kitty said, shooting me another wink.

Sophia shook her head. "Why did I pick that stupid name?"

"I kind of like it," Kitty said sweetly. She looked at me and mouthed the words, "Suits her to a T."

"What?" Sophia asked.

As if on cue, Aunt Edna barged into my bedroom. For the last two nights, my quarters had been taken over by Sophia as her sleeping chambers. This morning, my tiny pink bedroom was serving as the makeup and wardrobe department for act two of my plan—the fake funeral.

"Well, how do I look?" Aunt Edna asked. She'd tweezed her eyebrows, done her hair and makeup, and was donning a black silk dress that fit tight in all the right places.

I barely recognized her.

"Wow!" I said. "You look amazing!"

"You think?" she asked. "Kitty found this thing is the back of my closet. I haven't worn it since the Kennedy administration. Is the fur-lined cape-let too much?"

I shook my head. "No. Very Jackie O, if you ask me." I looked her up and down. "Full body girdle?"

Aunt Edna frowned. "How'd you know?"

I laughed. "Experience. All the celebrities wear them. And right now, you look a lot like one. Elizabeth Taylor, to be exact."

Aunt Edna's cheeks tinged rose. "I haven't heard that in a while. Are you just pulling my chain?"

I grinned. "Absolutely not."

"What do *you* think, Sophia?" Aunt Edna asked.

"How should I know?" the old woman grumbled, picking at her veil. "I couldn't see an *avalanche* coming through this thing."

"Edna, you never looked better," Kitty said. She beamed at her friend. "Necessity may be the mother of *invention*, but the mother of *reinvention* is romance. Believe me. You're gonna knock 'em dead at the funeral."

"Who's Edna gonna kill?" Jackie asked, appearing out of nowhere. She was dressed in a purple pantsuit quite possibly made from an old *Barney the Dinosaur* pelt.

"*Nobody*," Kitty said. "Edna's gonna win Morty over in this outfit. I'm telling you, one look and the man will be on his knees begging for another chance."

Aunt Edna frowned. "I wouldn't be so sure about that. Morty's no masochist, after all."

"What are you talking about?" Jackie said. "I seen him at mass last Sunday!"

• • • •

I WAS IN AUNT EDNA'S bedroom fixing a loose thread in the hem of her dress when Jackie popped her purple-hatted head in the doorframe and scared the bejeebers out of me.

"Hiya!" she announced, then slipped the rest of her wiry frame into the room.

"Geez, Jackie!" I squealed. "Give us some warning, would you? We're all kind of jumpy today."

"Sorry. I just wanted to let Edna know that Morty called. He said everything's all set."

Aunt Edna chewed her bottom lip. "Okay. Thanks, Jackie. Do me a favor? Go make sure Sophia isn't up to something?"

"On it, Capo." Jackie saluted, looking like an ancient stewardess for Flintstone Airways, and disappeared again.

I trimmed the loose thread at the bottom of Aunt Edna's dress. "Can I ask you something?"

My aunt shook her head. "Please. No more about me and Morty, okay? My nerves are shot as it is."

"No. That's not what I wanted—"

"You and Brady?" She shook her head at me. "I like him. Why are you wearing pants, Dorey? You should show him a little leg while you still got good gams."

I frowned. "I've got things to do today that a lady doesn't do in a dress, okay?"

Aunt Edna's tweezed eyebrow arched. "You don't say. So what did you want to ask me about?"

"What? Oh. It's about *Jackie*. I was wondering how she can be so ..."

"Addle brained and still drive?"

I laughed. "Well, that, too. But what I really want to know is how she can be so *stealthy*. That woman can pop up out of nowhere, and disappear just as quick."

"Oh." Aunt Edna shrugged. "Practice, I guess. It sure ain't camouflage. You've seen how she dresses. Jackie's outfits are loud enough to be charged with disturbing the peace."

I grinned. "True enough. So how does she do it?"

Aunt Edna adjusted her mink hat in the mirror. "I guess when you're wearing the opposite of camouflage, you learn other ways to blend into the crowd."

• • • •

"WOW! YOU LADIES LOOK beautiful," Brady said as Aunt Edna, Jackie, and Kitty paraded in front of him in their fancy funeral attire. "You all remind me of how my mom used to get us dressed up for Easter."

"Aww, that's sweet," Kitty said. "I guess with me in pink and Jackie in purple, we look like a couple of jellybeans."

Brady grinned. "No. You all look lovely. Especially you, Mrs. Barker." He wagged his eyebrows at her. "May I say, va-va-va-voom?"

"You may." Aunt Edna smiled shyly. "And call me Edna. By the way, Brady. I didn't want you to go hungry while you was watching the place. I made you some sandwiches to tide you over. They're in the icebox, along with a pitcher of iced tea and a whole apple pie."

Brady shot me a glance. "What? No *gingerbread*?"

"Gingerbread?" Aunt Edna cocked her head. "You like gingerbread?" She patted Brady's hand. "Next time, I promise. I'll have gingerbread."

I smirked at Brady. My cellphone buzzed. "Oh. My ride's here. I gotta go. See you all at the service, 12:30 sharp!"

"Why are you leaving so early?" Brady asked, following me to the front door.

I shrugged noncommittally. "I've just got a few little things to put into place before the crowds show up."

"Should I go with you?"

"No. I have plenty of reinforcements at the funeral home. Besides, nothing's going to happen there. It's all going to happen *here*, during the funeral service. That's why I need you to stay here with them until they're all safely underway."

Brady nodded. "Who's driving them?"

"Jackie." I glanced over at the skinny, septuagenarian dressed like a purple dinosaur. "Maybe you should say a prayer to St. Christopher, while you're at it."

"Who?"

"St. Christopher. The patron saint of travelers."

Chapter Forty-Six

As I approached the blue Ford Taurus, through the tinted window I could see Shirley Saurwein chewing her gum like a bottle-blonde cow.

"This had better be good," she said as I climbed into the passenger seat. "I'm missing a gopher race in Ruskin for this."

"It'll be worth it." I strapped on my seatbelt. "You'll see."

Saurwein hit the gas. "So you really think there's gonna be a mob showdown at your granny's fake funeral?"

"Doña Sophia Maria Lorenzo isn't my granny."

Wait a minute. Yes she is.

"So what's your connection with these gangsters, anyway?" Saurwein asked.

"Long-lost relatives."

She cackled. "You come to Florida for a visit, and they turn out to be mobsters. You just can't catch a break, can you Diller?"

I frowned. "I'm hoping to catch more than *a break* at the funeral, like I told you."

"Right. Some old mobster's just gonna show up and claim to be king of the Cornbread Cosa Nostra." Saurwein shook her head. "Diller, you may not be the dumbest chick in the world, but you better pray she doesn't die."

"There it is, up ahead," I said, pointing to an eggplant-colored Victorian mansion right off the interstate.

Saurwein hooked a right into the nearly empty parking lot of Neil Mansion Funeral Home. "I hope you're expecting a bigger crowd than this," she said, shifting into park. She grabbed her camera from the floorboard.

"You're going to have to leave that behind," I said. "It's too ... *obvious.*"

"What?" Saurwein hissed. "How am I supposed to get anything on video?"

"I've already got a professional crew on it. They're going to hide in the fake palms behind the casket and record the whole event. If anything juicy turns up, you've got first dibs."

Saurwein scowled. "There *better* be, for your sake, Diller. Or you're going right back to the top of my menu as *Jerk du Jour*."

"Believe me, there will be." I looked her up and down. "Thanks for wearing the black dress and orthopedic shoes. Now, just do everything like I say, and this could be the day your journalism career hits the big time."

• • • •

"WHAT AM I SUPPOSED to do in here?" Saurwein asked.

"Just look dead. In case somebody takes a peek."

I smirked. I had to admit, closing the coffin lid on Saurwein was like living out a fantasy that'd been knocking around in my head since the day I'd first met her. The sour, slightly frightened, distrustful look on her face as I covered it with a veil was one I'd savor until I took it to my *own* grave one day.

"Who's the woman in the coffin?" Kerri asked as walked over to her.

"Her? Just a problem I'm putting on layaway. Thanks for coming out and doing this for me so last minute."

"No. Thank *you*." Kerri cringed. "I owe you one after all that Crazy Eddie business. Plus, work's been slow. We're glad for the opportunity."

Kerri cupped her hand to her mouth and nodded in the direction of the young blond man setting up a camera tripod behind a screen of fake palms. "Marshall actually had to take a job as a DJ to pay the rent on the studio. Poor guy. He's been working day and night."

I frowned in sympathy. "I'm sorry things have been so slow. What about the money from the Crazy Eddie gig?"

Annoyance creased Kerri's normally pleasant face. "His wife Kareena refuses to pay us. In fact, she blames us for getting the public riled up. She says that's why someone killed Eddie. She's even threatened to sue us!"

"What?" I shook my head. "Geez. What a mess."

"I'm sorry," Kerri said. "This is *our* problem, not yours." She tried to put on a cheerful face. "So, what do you want us to do, exactly?"

"Well, mainly just stay up front here hidden behind all these fake palms and record whatever happens at the funeral."

"You want us to *hide*?"

"Well, yes. I don't want people getting stage fright, or acting weird because they know they're being recorded."

Kerri nodded. "I get that."

"Good. Now, tell Marshall to try and get headshots of everyone who comes in. And keep the camera panning around on the attendees, in case anything hinky goes down."

"Hinky?" Kerri asked.

"Yeah."

"What do you mean by—"

"Oh!" I blurted. "I gotta go. I need to talk to this guy coming in."

• • • •

"MORTY!" I SAID, SPRINTING over to meet the weary-looking baker standing at the front entrance to the funeral suite. I glanced at the sign-in table decorated with flowers and a picture of Sophia back in her heyday. "Nice. Is everything in place?"

"Yeah. We're good to go."

"Great." I hugged his neck. "You look good in a suit."

He grinned. "Thanks. Looks like we've got the same tailor."

I glanced down at my black pants and tennis shoes. "I know. But I need to be able to make a run for it in case things go down."

Morty sighed. "Don't we all."

"Good point." I glanced around. "Okay, let's get this show on the road, shall we?"

"Hold up a sec."

"What?"

Morty's eyes twinkled softly, looking out of place in his rugged, prize-fighter face. He smiled and nodded toward the sign-in table behind me. "Looking at you next to that picture of Sophia, I gotta say, you're a dead ringer for her at that age. Well, all except for the eyes. You've definitely got Sammy's eyes."

My heart fluttered. "You knew Sammy?"

"Yeah. And I've heard all the stories."

I looked down at my shoes again. "About him turning into a killing machine when he got drunk."

"Yeah." Morty reached out and touched my chin, then gently lifted it until my eyes met his. "But those were just gossip, Dorey. Sammy was a good man. Honest. The only problem he had was that he had too much integrity to make a good mobster. You know, Brady kind of reminds me of him, in that way."

My eyes brimmed with tears. "Really?"

"Yeah." Morty shook his head softly. "Sammy was head over heels about Maureen. He'd do anything for her." Morty locked eyes with me. "He *did* everything for her. *And* you."

"I want to know more," I said. "What about my mom? What was she like?"

"I'll tell you later. But right now, we've got a killer to catch, don't we?"

Chapter Forty-Seven

I breathed a sigh of relief when I saw the rusty old Kia pull into the funeral home parking lot at exactly 12:30. So far, my plan was running like clockwork. I rushed over to The Toad and yanked open the driver's door.

"You're right on time," I said, then found myself being licked in the face by Benny the pug. "What'd you bring the dog for?" I asked, wiping doggy saliva from my cheek.

"I couldn't leave her all alone at the apartments." Jackie climbed out of the driver's seat with the ancient old pug tucked in her arms. "Benny's too blind to find the doggy door anymore. Plus, she gets scared when she's left by herself."

"Uh ... okay." I felt uneasy, sensing a slight hitch might be developing in my plan. I scurried over to the passenger door to help Sophia out.

"I can do it," Sophia grumbled. "I'm not an invalid!"

"My Queenpin," I said, "from this point forward, no talking, please. At least, not in English. You're Brunhilda from Sicily, remember? We can't have your cover blown."

Sophia obliged by rattling off something in Italian.

"What did she say?" I asked Aunt Edna as she and Kitty climbed out of the back seats.

Aunt Edna shook her head. "Believe me. You don't want to know."

• • • •

WITH SOPHIA ON MY ARM, we entered the main door of Neil Mansion Funeral Home. Morty was waiting for us at the reception table. When he saw Aunt Edna, his practiced smile hit a glitch.

"Edna?" he asked, his mouth unable to shut.

"What?" she grumbled. "You sayin' you don't recognize me?"

Morty grinned. "I do *now*." He held out a crooked elbow. "May I escort a lady to her seat?"

A few steps behind my aunt, Jackie started to say something. Kitty slapped a hand over her mouth.

"You may," Aunt Edna said, and took Morty's arm. The pair smiled at each other, then began to make their way down the aisle toward the front of the suite reserved for Sophia's funeral.

"All the way up front," I called to them. "I reserved the first row for us."

"I don't see anybody here," Sophia complained, peeking out of her veil as we headed up the aisle.

"It's early," I said. "I wanted you in place before anyone else showed up."

Sophia grunted. "Humph. I'd say, 'We'll see about that,' but I'm as blind as a bat with this fakakta veil on."

I patted her gnarled hand. "Don't worry about that. Like I told you, we're recording everything. You'll get to see it all later." I sat Sophia down in the front row. "Now, please. No turning around and glaring at people. If you do, you could jeopardize the whole operation."

Sophia replied in Italian. Whatever she said, I figured I didn't want to know.

• • • •

AT A FEW MINUTES TO one o'clock, Neil Neil, the oddly named owner of Neil Mansion, made his way to the podium. The crowd was sparse. I was glad Sophia couldn't see.

Maybe I should've had Jackie spread gossip about the free food afterward ...

I noted a few familiar faces from Sophia's centennial birthday party. It seemed like an eternity ago, but shockingly, I counted a mere *five days* since the event. Even so, I couldn't place the names of the stranger anymore. I guess that old saying was true; babies and seniors mostly all looked alike.

There were a few attendees, however, who stood out from the crowd. I instantly recognized the tall, Lurch-like visage of Victor Ventura. He and Morty had carried the fake body bag to his hearse. And, of course, Morty himself. He was sitting beside Victor with his eyes glued on Edna, a goofy grin on his face.

There was also a skinny guy with a big nose and frizzy red hair who looked vaguely familiar. He'd been at the funeral of Freddy Sanderling last week. Freddy had been Sophia's food taster at the nursing home. He'd also been one of the seniors scammed by that iguana-toting Melanie Montoya.

I frowned, trying to remember the guy's name. He'd told me he was an attorney. He'd even given me his business card. I tried to picture it in my mind. His name was something weird.

Fargo? Ferris? Ferrolman?

"A-*hem*," Neil Neil said, startling me as he loudly cleared his throat into the podium microphone. "Thank you all for coming today on such ... *short notice*."

On those last two words, Neil Neil shot me and Aunt Edna some serious side-eye. Then the persnickety funeral director went on to deliver an overtly snarky speech about Sophia's life. It was peppered with puns such as "her un*time*ly demise," and "her *short time* with us," leaving me in no doubt as to how put-out he felt for having to arrange such a hasty funeral.

"I'll conclude with this *brief* word," Neil Neil said. "Though *short* in stature, Sophia Lorenzo will be remembered for a *long time*." He nodded his head curtly, then said, "I'll now turn the microphone over to anyone who would like to say a few *timely* words. Afterward, everyone is invited to retire to the salon for refreshments."

Neil took a step away from the podium. A female voice rang out from the back of the room.

"I've got something to say!"

I turned my head and spotted a woman in the back row waving her hand like a kid in class who desperately needed to pee. I hadn't noticed her come in. But when she stood and approached the podium, the busty, auburn-haired woman in a clingy red dress seemed hauntingly familiar.

"Not this chick again," I heard Aunt Edna mutter.

I elbowed Jackie. "Is that—?"

"Victoria Polaski," Jackie said.

I grimaced. "The one Sophia calls Slick?"

"The very one."

As Slick wiggled past us in the aisle, Benny growled in Jackie's arms. I frowned.

That can't be a good sign.

The microphone crackled as "Slick" blew her nose into it, then dabbed the same hanky at her thickly mascaraed eyes. "Scotty and I were very close," she whimpered. "Nobody knew it, but we were secretly engaged."

"What kind of horse hockey is this?" Sophia yelled.

Startled, Neil Neil scrambled forward and took the microphone from Slick. "Um, excuse me, *Miss Scarlet*. This is the funeral for *Sophia Lorenzo*. Scotty McBride's funeral is going on in the next suite over."

"Oh." Slick sniffed and looked down her powdered nose at us. "Oops. My bad." Her crocodile tears evaporated. She smiled, curtseyed, and waved at us like a two-bit starlet at a low-budget movie premiere.

"What a piece of work," Aunt Edna said, scowling and shaking her head.

As Slick flounced past us down the aisle, Benny started barking her little pug head off. "I told you she smells deadbeats," Jackie said, smiling down at Benny like a proud mama.

"One thing's for sure," Kitty said. "Slick sure got *Edna* seeing red."

I glanced over at Aunt Edna. Her face was the color of a ripe tomato.

"Red," I said absently.

The color of danger.

I leapt up out my chair. "Excuse me. I've got to go!"

"What?" Kitty asked. "Why?"

"No time to explain. Stay here with the others." I scooted to the end of the row and sprinted halfway down the aisle.

But that was as far as I got.

Out of nowhere, a figure came barreling right for me. It was someone I hadn't planned on.

Not even in Plan C.

Chapter Forty-Eight

I stood frozen in the aisle as Monkey-Face Mongo hurtled toward me. Dressed in a gangster's pinstripe suit, he cradled a long, narrow box under one arm. A box the perfect size and shape to house a Chicago typewriter—aka a Tommy gun.

As Mongo drew nearer, I could see the lunatic gleam shining from his semi-primate eyes. "Ack!" was all I managed to utter as Mongo rushed toward me, tearing open the box.

"Edna!" he yelled. "Edna Barker! Where are you?"

Mongo swooshed past me, flinging the empty box behind him. "Edna! I know you're in here!"

As if in slow motion, I watched my aunt stand and turn around to face the escaped convict.

My voice failing me, I mouthed the word, "No!" Then I noticed something that made my heart melt.

Aunt Edna didn't look frightened. She smiled at me softly, then shifted her gaze to Mongo as she worked her way to the aisle. The calm, resolute expression on her beautiful face told me she'd resigned herself to her fate.

"I'm right here, Marco," Aunt Edna said.

Mongo stopped in his tracks. "Ah! There you are!" He rushed up to Edna and shoved something at her. "This is for you!"

I caught a flash of red.

Oh my god! Is that a bayonet?

My voice cracked as I screamed, "No!"

Then, as if my single word had the power of a .45 caliber bullet, I saw Monkey-Face Mongo go down on one knee.

"Marry me, Edna!" he said. "I can't wait no longer!"

My own knees almost buckled. The bayonet wasn't a bayonet. It was a dozen long-stemmed red roses. I stared, dumbfounded, as my aunt held them in her hands like a bridal bouquet.

Marco Telleroni didn't want to murderize my aunt. He wanted to *marry* her!

"Hold on there just a minute!" Morty's voice boomed from the dead silence of the funeral suite.

Mongo turned around. "Is that you, Morty?"

"You're damned right it's me!"

"Well, you're too late!" Mongo said as Morty marched toward him. "All these years, you had your chance with Edna here. But like a fool, you wasted it!"

For a moment, the two men glared at each other, nose-to-nose, like a pair of feuding mountain gorillas.

"Men, please!" Aunt Edna said. A coy smile curled her lips. "Continue."

Taking his cue, Morty took a swing at Marco. He missed and fumbled sideways. As he struggled to regain his balance, Marco scrambled to the podium.

Mongo grabbed the microphone and sneered at Morty. He opened his mouth and was about to say what I figured would be some rather unflattering words about Morty.

But the grizzled old baker never gave him the chance. A right hook sent Mongo's bridgework flying. The two seized hold of each other and grappled and scuffled around until they both fell to the ground.

Mongo dropped the microphone. It tumbled to the floor beside them, amplifying every grunt and groan the two men made as they wrestled around. Realizing they were on mic, the two men lost focus and struggled back to their feet.

That's when someone yelled, "Call the police!"

Mongo's eyes grew wide. He turned and scanned the crowd to see who might be dialing the cops. Morty seized the opportunity and clocked Mongo on the side of his primate noggin. Knocked out cold, Mongo tumbled backward, striking the coffin like a 250-pound sack of potatoes.

Knocked off its pedestal, the coffin careened to the floor and burst open. Shirley Saurwein came rolling out. Either she was unconscious or she was a damned good actress. She came to rest lying face down in the ugly red carpet.

"Look at that!" someone yelled. "Sophia sure has let herself go!"

• • • •

"HAS ANYBODY SEEN KERRI?" I asked, scrambling around in the ensuing mayhem. Morty had Mongo pinned into a corner, tying his arms behind his back with his own necktie. Neil Neil was running around, shrieking in panic, looking as if he's just escaped from prison himself.

"Kerri?" I shouted into the crowd.

"Is that the name of the woman in red?" a man's voice asked behind me. I turned around and came nose-to-nose with the frizzy-haired attorney from Freddy's funeral.

I frowned. "What are *you* doing here?"

He smirked. "Not *this* routine again. Don't you remember? I'm an attorney. Just looking to drum up a little business."

He handed me his card. I read it aloud. "Ferrol Finkerman. You just don't give things a rest, do you?"

He raised an auburn eyebrow. "You either, apparently. What's your dealio?"

"Dealio?"

"Yeah. Your scheme. Your game." Finkerman rubbed shoulders with me. "Maybe we can work together."

I snarled. "Over my dead body!"

"How poetic." Finkerman shrugged. "Have it your way. You're not my first turn-down of the day."

"What?" I gasped. "Are you harassing these people?"

"Me?" Finkerman looked taken aback. "Compared to that redhead's act, I'm the Pope. That gal might not be too bright, but she's sure got herself a clever manager."

My brow furrowed. "What are you talking about?"

"After she brushed me off, I heard her leaving a message for someone on her cellphone." Finkerman laughed. "Whoever it was didn't take her call. Boy, she ripped him a new one."

"Did she happen to say anyone's name?"

"No. But based on the choice terms of endearment she used, I'd bet it was her soon-to-be-ex-husband."

Finkerman wagged his eyebrows at me, then disappeared in the crowd. I tried to follow him, but then I spotted who I'd been looking for in the first place.

"Kerri!" I called out, working my way toward her and Marshall. "Did you guys get all that on tape?"

Marshall shot me a thumb's up. "Yep! It was wicked!"

"Uh ... right." I spotted Morty holding Aunt Edna's hand. Suddenly I felt as if maybe something good would come of this fiasco yet.

"It *was* pretty wicked, wasn't it?" I said. "Now, listen carefully. I need you two to get a video of that woman lying over there."

"The one that fell out of the coffin?" Kerri asked.

"Yes. Move that veil out of her face and get some video of her by the coffin. And make sure that bridgework on the carpet beside her makes it into the shot."

"What do you want the video for?" Marshall asked.

I smirked. "Insurance purposes. When she comes to, give her a thumb drive of the video you make of her by the coffin. Let her think it's the footage from the entire funeral, compliments of me."

Kerri's brow furrowed. "Okay, but—"

I shook my head. "Look, I'll explain it all later. But right now, I gotta go. Remember, whatever you do, *don't* give that woman any of the other footage, okay?"

Marshall nodded. “Got it.”

“Where are you going in such a hurry?” Kerri asked.

“To where the real action is. I think I just figured out what’s really going on here.”

Chapter Forty-Nine

I screeched up in front of Palm Court Cottages in The Toad. Like a prince from a fairytale, it had cranked on the first try. "I'd kiss you," I said, patting the dashboard, "but I'm afraid I might catch something."

Brady stepped out of the hedges in front of Aunt Edna's apartment and sprinted toward me. "What's going on?" he asked. "Is everything okay?"

"Yes." I slammed the door and met him on the sidewalk. "What about here? Any action?"

"Nothing yet."

"I'd say it's been a total bust," a man's voice said. His head popped up above the top of the hedges.

I gasped. "Sergeant McNulty! What are *you* doing here?"

He lowered his mirrored shades and shot me a sour look. "How could I pass up the opportunity to spend my day off swatting mosquitos and hiding in azalea bushes?"

"I asked him to back me up," Brady said. "In case this turned out to be a worse-case scenario."

"But—"

"He's right," McNulty said. "With you, Diller, "it's *always* a worse-case scenario."

I frowned. "I'll have you know I led a fairly normal life before I started stabbing people on TV."

"A vehicle's coming," Brady said. "Everybody take cover."

The three of us scrambled into the hedges and crouched down. A white Ford Transit van with tinted windows drove slowly by, obviously scoping out the place.

"Get in position," McNulty said, peering through binoculars. "They're turning around. Who're we looking for, Diller?"

"Humpty ... uh ... Humphrey Bogaratelli. I called and left him an anonymous tip that there was a ton of cash stashed in Sophia's mattress."

"That's entrapment!" McNulty said.

I grimaced. "Even if there's no money in the mattress?"

"Then it's not entrapment—it's stupidity." McNulty shook his head, then returned to peering through the bushes with the binoculars. "Description of the suspect?"

"Uh ... money-runner. Poisoner. Two-timing bast—"

He turned and shot me a look. "I meant *physical* description."

"Oh. Um ... bald. Sixty-something. Beer belly. Five-foot two, three maybe?"

McNulty let out a breath. "Charming."

"Hush," Brady said. "Someone's getting out of the van."

"Whoever it is doesn't fit the description," McNulty said.

"What? Lemme see." I snatched the binoculars from him and trained them on the person approaching the sidewalk. I couldn't believe my eyes. Coming up the walk was a tall, thin person in a hoodie. They were carrying a duffle bag. And they had a cleft chin.

"You know who it is?" Brady asked.

I shook my head. "No."

"Probably a false alarm," McNulty said. "Some millennial handing out flyers to a tattoo and vape festival."

"Just give them a minute," I said. "See if they break into Sophia's place. It's the only way to catch them red-handed."

"Been watching *Murder She Wrote* again?" McNulty quipped, snatching the binoculars back.

Suddenly, the person in the hoodie stopped in their tracks. They turned and looked our way. The three of us froze, not daring to take a breath.

After a moment, the hooded figure turned and headed right for Sophia's apartment. A few seconds later, I heard the sound of glass breaking.

"Let's go," McNulty said.

I grabbed his arm. "Not yet. I need them to take the bait."

"What bait?" Brady asked. "I thought you said there wasn't any money in Sophia's mattress."

"Did I? I meant, there wasn't *very much* money."

McNulty shook his head. "If this wasn't potentially tied to a murder investigation, right about now I'd be kicking both of your rotten heads in."

"Don't move."

"Where am I gonna go?" I asked.

I scowled at Brady and McNulty, then suddenly realized that neither of them had uttered the command.

It was a third man. And he was pointing a gun right at us.

Chapter Fifty

"Who're your pals here?" Humphrey Bogaratelli asked, training his revolver on us.

"Uh ... they're my brothers," I lied.

"One black, one white, eh? Your mamma must've gotten around."

"I got it!" a male voice rang out from the courtyard.

That's when I realized the figure in the hoodie was a man. He was slowly working his way down the garden path, dragging a duffle bag stuffed to the gills.

"Look, you've got the cash," I said. "Just leave. Nobody's stopping you."

"Hold up a sec," Humpty said. "It was *you* who tipped me off about the mattress, wasn't it. Why'd you do it?"

"I just wanted you to leave Sophia alone. She's old. She'll die soon enough."

Humpty's pudgy face lost its smugness. "I thought she already *did*."

"Oh." I swallowed hard. "About that ..."

"Come on, Dad!" the young man called out. He brushed the hoodie aside. Sweat streamed down his face. "I need your help. It's too heavy!"

"Hold on!" Humpty yelled. "Can't you see I'm a little busy here?"

"But Dad!"

Annoyed, Humpty took a glance toward his son.

"Go," McNulty whispered.

All of a sudden, everything around me became a blur of motion. A gunshot rang out. I could feel the heat of the bullet as it passed mere inches from my face. I heard a metallic *clink*. Then a man yelped.

What the hell's going on?

By the time I could get my bearings, Brady was on top of Humpty, pinning him to the ground.

"Damn it, Racer!" Humpty yelled. His hand that had been aiming the revolver at us was now empty and bleeding.

I heard a vehicle engine start. I scrambled off my knees and stood up. Over the hedges, I saw the young man running toward the van. McNulty was on his tail, about five yards behind him.

"I've got this guy," Brady said. "Go help McNulty!"

Without thinking, I grabbed Humpty's gun from the ground and ran after McNulty. I heard a shot fire and a tire blowout. As I stepped into the road for a better view, I spotted the white van barreling right for me.

Unable to get my feet to move, I stood my ground, squeezed my eyes almost shut, and shot at the van until the gun emptied.

As the smoke cleared, I heard another gunshot—and another tire blow. A sharp creak pierced the air as the back end of the van sunk a foot. Smoke began billowing from the front grille, then the engine died. The van stalled out and rolled to a stop in the middle of the road six feet in front of me.

Through the blown-out windshield, I made out the face of the person behind the wheel. It was Kareena Houser. A Virginia Slim hung limp from the corner of her open mouth. In the passenger seat beside her sat another familiar face. Her other son, the ScarBux delivery kid named Chase.

We stared at each other, all too stunned to move. My mind began to whir as it put pieces together like a jigsaw puzzle.

"Some help here," I heard McNulty groan.

"Nobody move!" I yelled, suddenly coming back to life. I trained the empty gun on the van as I cautiously made my way to the side of the vehicle. McNulty was limping alongside it. Blood was running down his pant leg.

"McNulty!" I gasped. "What happened?"

"A bull gored me, Diller. What do you *think*? Call an ambulance!"

• • • •

"SHOT IN THE BUTT," McNulty said as he was wheeled into the ambulance on a stretcher. "Why is it always the sergeant who gets it in the end?"

"You're gonna be all right," the EMT said. "Looks like the bullet passed clean through without hitting any major arteries."

"But it's still going to be a pain in the ass, isn't it?" McNulty said, his eyes locked with mine.

"Oh, you'll feel it all right," the EMT said. "Just as soon as the morphine wears off."

McNulty shook his head. "You just can't stay out of trouble, can you Diller?"

I winced out a sympathetic smile. "Sorry."

"You'll be okay, Sarge," Brady said.

"I suppose," McNulty said.

Relieved, I gawked in wonder at the flashing lights and cops surrounding Palm Court Cottages. I looked up at Brady. "You guys really have each other's backs, don't you?"

"We have to." Brady turned to McNulty. "I'll come check on you at the hospital as soon as we get these people booked."

"You do that," McNulty said. "And bring Diller with you."

"Why?" I asked.

"You shot me. You're going to have to deal with that."

Chapter Fifty-One

"I think I know what happened," I said to Brady as he drove us to the police station. "It all makes sense now."

Brady shook his head. "Well, that makes one of us. Fill me in. Who was the woman driving the van?"

"Kareena Houser. Eddie Houser's wife."

"The dead guy? How's *she* tied up in all this?"

"By blood. Those two young men with her are her sons, Racer and Chase."

Brady shook his head. "No wonder they turned to a life of crime."

"Yeah. It gets better. The kids aren't Eddie's. They're Humphrey Bogaratelli's. The young guy in the hoodie called Humpty 'Dad.' You heard him yourself."

Brady hooked a left onto Fourth Street. "So Bogaratelli was messing around with Kareena on the side and Eddie found out about it?"

"Yes. I think they were able to keep their affair under wraps for a long time. But when Eddie found out, they decided he had to go. Humpty whacked Eddie and tried to frame me for it."

"Why?"

"As far as I can figure, he needed the money."

"But I thought you said Humpty was in control of the Family Fund."

"He was. For over thirty years. But having three wives uses up a lot of cash."

Brady nearly wrecked the patrol car. "Wait. *What*?"

"Three women," I said. "I figured it out when I was talking to Ferrol Finkerman at the funeral."

"Ferrol who?"

"Long story. Not important right now. Anyway, you know how you and I thought Melanie Montoya had a partner in scamming those old folks in the nursing home? Getting them to hand over control of their assets by signing powers of attorney?"

Brady shot me a glance. "Yeah."

"Montoya's partner had to be *Humpty*. With power of attorney over Sophia, they could grab all the assets she had *legally*. We foiled their plans, so they had to switch up their game."

"Okay," Brady said. "But how—"

"The way I figure, Humpty is either married to Melanie or shacking up with her. He was always going down to Boca Raton. She's got a place down there. It's a lot easier to hide another wife if she's out of town, right? Plus, why would she drive all the way from Boca to bring therapy animals to a nursing home in St. Pete?"

"And this Ferrol guy told you all this?"

"No." I shook my head. "You missed the big fireworks at the funeral. At the end of the service, this piece of work named Victoria Polanski went up to the podium and started running the same fake fiancé scam she did at Freddy Sanderling's funeral. Only she got the *wrong* funeral."

"What?"

"Yeah. Finkerman told me he heard her on her cellphone blessing out some guy for not answering his phone. He told me it sounded to him like she was talking to her *soon-to-be ex-husband*."

"And you think that soon-to-be-ex was Humpty ... I mean Humphrey Bogaratelli?"

"It sure fits his M.O. Find a woman dumb enough and greedy enough to help him run his scams. And he seems to have a thing for redheads."

"Melanie is blonde," Brady said.

"Bottle job. Anybody can tell that. Take a look at her roots next time you pass her jail cell."

"So let's say you're right. Humpty's running a shell game with three different women. Why should it blow up now?"

"Two reasons. Okay, everything's been running smoothly for years. Humpty's got it made, having these women do his dirty work. He thinks he's untouchable. So he ups his game."

"How?"

"He has Eddie start helping him with things. Aunt Edna told me she thought Humpty and Eddie might've been working in cahoots to steal from the Family Fund."

"Seriously?" Brady shook his head. "Who *isn't* in on this?"

"I know, right? Anyway, Humpty's all of a sudden more and more in the picture, hanging around Kareena and the kids. Maybe Eddie starts to notice things."

"What kind of things?"

"That maybe Kareena likes Humpty too much. Or that now that Racer and Chase are young men, Eddie spots a family resemblance, only it's not to *him*."

"I see." Brady chewed his bottom lip. "Or maybe one of those boys slipped up and called Humpty 'Dad.' They don't seem like the brightest bulbs in the carton."

"Exactly. Maybe Kareena and Humpty get nervous. They start worrying Eddie's going to put two and two together and come up with TNT."

"Huh?"

"Blow his top. Seek revenge. So together, Humpty and Kareena conspire to get rid of Eddie before he can get rid of either of them."

"And the second thing?" Brady asked. "You said you had two reasons why you thought the gig was up for Humpty."

"Oh. The Family Fund. Morty told me Humpty had drained it dry. He needed a big score if he was going to keep his shell game running."

"Thus the money in the mattress," Brady said.

I smiled. "Bingo."

Brady pulled into the police station and parked. "That all makes sense, Doreen. But why would Humpty try to pin Eddie's murder on you?"

"I dunno." I unbuckled my seat belt. "But that's what I'd like to find out."

Chapter Fifty-Two

"Please," I whined. I'd followed Brady through the police station all the way to booking, but he wouldn't let me go with him to the interrogation room. "Give me a few minutes with Kareena. I think I know how to get her to talk."

"She's already told Officer Daniels she won't talk to a cop."

I smiled. "I'm not a cop. I'm a rival. And if I know Kareena like I think I do, she just might be spoiling for a catfight."

Brady frowned. "Doreen, I'm not going to let you sit alone with a murder suspect."

"I won't be alone. You'll be behind the glass watching, and I'll be armed with a pack of Virginia Slims."

"I dunno."

"Gimme one crack at her, Brady. If you do, I'll tell you who scratched PIG into the side of your truck."

Brady pursed his lips. "Okay. You got five minutes."

• • • •

"I KNEW IT!" KAREENA said, sucking on a Virginia Slim like it was going to save her soul. "I knew Humpty was getting' some strange with a chick down in Boca Raton. Lousy cheater."

That's rich, considering you were married to Eddie.

"Melanie wasn't the only one," I said.

"What?" Kareena eyed me up and down. "I guess you'd know all about that, wouldn't you? You've been trying to break up my marriage since you laid eyes on Eddie."

"Excuse me?" I said.

"I saw Eddie making eyes at you. Squeezing your ass during that stupid commercial. And I found a copy of that contract on his desk. He was gonna give you a Nissan Cube." Kareena snarled and shook her head. "That's Eddie's classic MO. Give a girl a free ride, then pull the wool over her eyes."

"So he's done this before?" I offered her another cigarette.

Kareena grabbed it and let out a long sigh. "Since we first got hitched. You were just the last in a long string of trashy bimbos. You know, the whole ironical thing about this is, we'd have had a legit fortune if it weren't for his wandering eye."

Ironical? What about your own?

"That must've hurt," I said. "But believe me, I wasn't going to take Eddie's deal."

Kareena cocked her head. "You were gonna do it for *free*?"

"What? No. I mean ... I have a *boyfriend*. I wouldn't cheat on him."

"Oh. You mean the pig? He's kinda cute. You know, for a pig."

"Er ... so Kareena, who killed Eddie?"

Kareena sighed and stamped out her cigarette butt. "Racer did it." She shook her head. "Humpty filled him with tales about how he knew where this fortune was hidden. That all they had to do was go steal it, and we could all leave Eddie's stupid used car business behind."

"Where was the fortune?"

"Some old lady hoarder had it," she said. "He didn't tell us who. Humpty had tried to get the old lady to die so he could get it without nobody knowing about it. He'd planned it for months. But then last week, he told me something went wrong. He had to adjust the plan."

"What plan?"

"To kill the old lady and get her fortune," Kareena said. "Pay attention!"

"Sorry." I offered her another cigarette. She took it.

"Humpty told Racer about the setback. That it might take a few more weeks to get things in place. But Racer, our oldest, ain't the most patient kid in the world. He and Eddie never got along. He was tired of having to work at Eddie's car lot. He thought it was degrading. So when Humpty told us his plans were gonna take longer than he thought, Racer lost it."

"He killed Eddie."

"Yeah. He told Humpty. He blew a gasket! But Humpty told Racer not to worry. He'd make it all go away. And he did. The next day, you showed up for that stupid sale of the century at the car lot, and Eddie didn't."

"Humpty set it up to make it look like I murdered Eddie. Why?"

Kareena smiled cruelly. "Because I told him to. He needed a patsy, and I needed revenge."

• • • •

"GEEZ, DILLER. I'VE got to hand it to you," Brady said as I walked out of the room with Kareena. "You really got that woman to open up."

I smiled smugly. "Weren't expecting a full-blown confession, eh?"

"Well, at this point, Kareena's only pointed the blame at her son and Humpty. We're going to need some corroborating evidence to make it stick. Any ideas?"

"Yeah. Ask her other son, Chase."

Brady cocked his head. "Ask him *what*, exactly?"

"Have him tell you about ScarBux."

Chapter Fifty-Three

After assembling a list of questions for Brady, it was my turn to sit behind the mirror and watch as Brady interviewed a terrified young man who was barely out of his teens.

The youngest offspring of Kareena Houser and Humphrey Bogaratelli appeared totally unaware of his parents' criminal intents.

"How did you get involved in ScarBux?" Brady asked.

Chase fiddled with his fingers and chewed his bottom lip. "Dad told me I needed a part-time job to start building experience. You know, to put on a job application."

"Sure," Brady said. "That makes sense. So, why ScarBux?"

"It was Dad's idea. He actually started the company. He wants ... *wanted* me to be an entrepreneur."

"How did the company work?"

"Dad made the coffee in the morning, and I delivered it."

Brady nodded. "So, what kind of hours did you work?"

Chase shrugged. "Not many. I have morning classes at the junior college. I didn't have time to find customers. Dad found me my first one."

"The old woman at Palm Court Cottages?"

"Yeah. Sophia." Chase looked up at Brady, his eyes brimming with tears. "I didn't know we were going to rob her!"

"It's okay," Brady said. "You're not being charged with that. I'm just trying to find out about ScarBux."

"I thought it was legit," Chase said. "Dad had cups printed up and everything."

"What about the sugar packets?" Brady asked.

"Dad bought them at a restaurant supply store. He had a rubber stamp made. I stamped the name on the packets and left them to dry. Dad put them into baggies for me to give to the old lady."

"How long have you been delivering coffee to her?"

"A couple of months."

"Good. Now, Chase, do you happen to still have any of the sugar packets?"

"Dad told me to throw them all away. He didn't need them anymore."

"Oh," Brady sighed.

Chase shrugged. "But I forgot." He reached into a pocket and pulled out a baggie of packets. "Is this what you're looking for?"

"Yes, it absolutely is," Brady said.

As I'd instructed, Brady let the baggie lie on the table untouched. He shot me a covert thumbs up. Then he turned to the frightened young man and said, "Thanks, Chase. That's all for now."

• • • •

"GOOD WORK," I SAID to Brady, meeting him in the interrogation room after Chase left. "Just as I suspected, ScarBux was another one of Humpty's scams."

A lab tech arrived suited up with rubber gloves.

"Take those for testing," Brady said. "Handle them carefully."

"You got it." As the tech picked the baggie up with a pair of tongs, Humpty passed by in handcuffs on his way to booking.

"Hey, Humpty!" I said, shooting him a grin. "Look what we found. We'll be sure to test them for thallium."

Humpty glanced at the packets. His pudgy face went pale. "Those aren't mine. I'm being framed!"

"Gee," I said. "I wouldn't have any idea how *that* feels."

• • • •

"SO WHO SCRATCHED PIG into my truck?" Brady asked. We were sitting at his desk eating Dairy Hog hamburgers and filling out a mountain of paperwork big enough to give a Billy goat indigestion.

"Racer," I said, sucking down a sip of vanilla milkshake. "I saw him in the street at Sundial. When he pulled that hoodie off in the courtyard today, I was sure it was him."

Brady shook his head. "But why?"

"You're asking *me* why criminals do the things they do?"

Brady laughed. "Good point."

I shrugged. "Actually, I think it might've been jealousy. Kareena thought Eddie and I were having an affair. He grabbed my ass, you know."

Brady frowned. "Good thing he's dead."

I grinned. "Jealous, are we?"

Brady blew out a breath. "I'm too tired to be jealous. Now, help me concentrate." He turned over a form he was filling out. "According to the evidence report, the money seized in the duffle turned out to be mostly ones and fives wrapped around stacks of blank paper."

I smirked. "You don't say."

Brady shot me a look. "Humpty's treasure hunt turned out to be worth less than three hundred dollars."

"That's a crying shame."

"Doreen, the banknotes are going to have their serial numbers traced. If they're part of a bank heist or something, that could open up a whole new can of worms for your family."

I pictured me and the other mob molls sitting around Aunt Edna's dining table sipping tea, eating snickerdoodles, and wrapping the fake money bundles with small notes Morty had brought us from his bakery business.

"I'm not worried about that," I said.

The look of relief on Brady's face was precious. "Good. So answer me this one last thing. Why thallium? And why sugar packets?"

I shrugged. "As my Aunt Edna always says, "Revenge is a dish best served in a disposable container."

Chapter Fifty-Four

"You got home late last night," Aunt Edna said, poking her head into my bedroom.

"Yeah. Thanks for the clean sheets. And for getting Sophia out of my bed."

"Oh, that was the easy part." Aunt Edna laughed. "When she saw the new memory foam mattress being delivered, she practically stampeded over me to check it out."

I grinned. "I wish I'd been there to see it."

"Oh, from what I hear, you saw *plenty* yesterday. Now get dressed and come to breakfast. We're all dying to hear how everything turned out."

• • • •

"SERIOUSLY? HUMPTY HAD *three wives*?" Kitty nearly spilled her coffee. "The man looks like a boiled egg with legs!"

"What a trio of bimbos *they* had to be," Sophia said. "I don't think even Oscar Mayer could swallow that much baloney. Still, it's a shame ScarBux was a sham. Humpty could sure make some good coffee."

I glanced over at Aunt Edna. She didn't appear to have heard Sophia's slight. She was too busy gazing into Morty's eyes while he returned the favor.

"I hate to break up a pair of love birds," I said. "But Morty, you told us Humpty nearly emptied the Family Fund trying to cover his own expenses. How come we kept receiving enough money to get by on?"

Morty shrugged. "It's a mystery."

Aunt Edna's mouth fell open. "It was *you*, wasn't it? *You* paid the rent and kept a roof over our heads!"

"Hey," Sophia grumbled. "I coughed up a few bucks as needed, too, you know. Not all those bills were traceable."

"The truth is, this place has been paid off for years," Morty said. "I was going through some papers in Humpty's car last night. The mortgage on Palm Court Cottages is free and clear. And it's in Sophia's name."

"Geez," I said. "If Humpty had managed to get that power of attorney, we'd all be out on the street. He'd have sold this place right out from under us."

"I guarantee it," Morty said.

"Well, Humpty won't have to worry about food and shelter where he's going," Jackie said. "I only hope there's worms in his porridge, like in *Shawshank Redemption*."

I grinned at Jackie. "Precisely."

Morty laughed. "You know, while I was waiting for the cops to come take Mongo away, he told me Humpty framed him for murder."

My nose crinkled. "Really? Wouldn't it be the ultimate karma if fate made them cellmates?"

"It sure would," Sophia said. "Humpty wanted to have big money. Turns out he only had a big mouth. Let's see how that works out for him in prison."

"Speaking of money, it's Monday," Kitty said. "Has anyone checked the Family Fund account?"

"I'll do it." Morty pulled out his cellphone. "That body bag full of bills Victor deposited at the bank Saturday should have registered in our new account by now." He grinned and wagged his eyebrows. "I think we just might be looking at a tidy sum."

"Hey, look at all the zeroes!" Jackie said, peeking over his shoulder.

Morty's jaw dropped. "There's *only* zeroes. The account's *empty*."

"Awe, geez!" Aunt Edna said. "Don't tell me we've been conned ourselves!"

"*Now* I think I know who sent the flowers," Kitty said, shaking her head. "Victor Polanski, you dirty, double-crossing dog!"

Chapter Fifty-Five

"I can't believe Victor would do that!" Morty said. "He told me I had nothing to worry about. That I could trust him!"

"How could you make such an amateur mistake, Morty?" Aunt Edna said. "Smart people don't tell you how smart they are. Rich people don't tell you how rich they are. Honest people don't tell you how honest they are. Only con men do!"

"Humpty needed all that money to support his girlfriends and wives," Jackie said. "Maybe Victor has a whole harem, too!"

Kitty shook her head in disgust. "And he had the nerve to show up at your fake funeral, too, Sophia! That smirk on his face. I should've known he was up to something!"

"It's all dirty money," Sophia said. "From a Federal bank heist. If Victor tries to use them, he'll be busted faster than a cheap party balloon. That's why I never spent the dough in the first place."

"But why let us try to deposit it, then?" Aunt Edna asked.

Sophia smirked and adjusted the silver turban on her head. "Because I knew it would never make it to a bank. Look around! Haven't you all noticed? Everybody we know is a con man!"

Kitty sighed. "I guess you're right."

"I *know* I'm right," Sophia said. "Besides, I was tired of sleeping on that lumpy mattress. Thirty years was enough."

Aunt Edna frowned. "I'm glad you can make jokes, Sophia. But it's not funny. We're broke."

"No we're not." Morty smiled. "We own the apartments. Given today's inflation, they're worth at least a half a million bucks."

"We could take out a home equity line on them," I said.

"No need for that." Sophia stood and started toddling toward the living room. "What are you all waiting for? Follow me."

The old Queenpin took up position in the "good chair"—Aunt Edna's ugly old brown vinyl recliner. "Gather round," she said as we filed in. "I've got something I want to tell you."

Morty opted to stand. We four ladies squeezed together into the olive-hued velveteen couch.

Sophia's cat-green eyes sparkled. "Now, what I'm about to tell you is my *last* secret."

"What was the first one?" Jackie asked.

Sophia rolled her eyes. "Pay attention. You're gonna like this. Especially you, Edna."

Aunt Edna's eyebrow rose with suspicion. "What do you mean?"

Sophia grinned like a Sphinx. "I'm finally granting you permission to get rid of this hideous chair."

"What?" Aunt Edna gasped. "I mean, thank you. I've been wanting to for thirty years! But why? Why *now*?"

"Because we're about to bust it open like a piñata," Sophia said. "There's a couple hundred grand in gold coins stuffed inside this bad boy."

Chapter Fifty-Six

I was on my way out the door when my phone rang. It was the call I'd been waiting for.

"Shirley Saurwein," I said smugly. "How's it hanging?"

"What's the meaning of this?" she hissed over the phone.

"I have no idea what you're talking about."

"The video of me passed out by the coffin!" Saurwein screeched. "Dear god. Whose *dentures* are those anyway?"

I stifled a laugh. "All I know is I heard a rumor about some two-bit reporter who faked her own death to try and make the national headlines. Poor dear passed out, pissed herself, and lost her dentures in the process. But like I said. It's just a rumor. The actual video hasn't been released yet."

"You wouldn't."

"Wouldn't what?" I asked sweetly.

"Unbelievable!" Saurwein hissed. "Blackmail? You really *are* related to the mob, aren't you, Diller?"

"All I want is to live in peace. How about you?"

"Ha," Saurwein laughed bitterly. "So you decided to answer the call of your family. Too bad it's 'Scam Likely.'"

"Hey, you're the one who taught me that the best way to make a lasting impression is with a sledge hammer."

Saurwein blew out a sigh. "Touché. Be seeing you Diller."

I smirked. "Not if I see you first."

I clicked off the phone.

"Who were you talking to?" Jackie asked, appearing out of nowhere with Benny in her arms.

"Oh, just a big nobody." I opened the front door and took a step outside.

"Where you off to?" Jackie asked.

I cringed. "I've got to go see a man about a bullet hole in his butt."

Jackie grinned. "I hate when that happens."

Chapter Fifty-Seven

"You ready?" Brady asked, meeting me outside the hospital room where Sergeant McNulty lay—though probably not on his back.

I cringed. "I guess so. I shot McNulty in the ass, Brady. What's he gonna do to me? Press charges?"

Brady shot me a sympathetic smile. "I don't know."

I blew out a breath and took a step toward McNulty's room. "Come on, let's get this over with."

"Nope. He wants to see you alone." Brady grimaced. "Good luck."

"Thanks." I pushed open the door. McNulty was lying on his side in the hospital bed. An IV drip ran to a vein in the crook of his elbow.

"Diller," he said, his voice husky and dry.

I rushed to his side. "I'm *so sorry*, Sergeant McNutly! I didn't mean to shoot you! I've never even fired a gun before!"

"No kidding," he quipped.

I winced. "You know, I normally lead an ordinary, mundane life. It's just that lately, it's been ... you know ... sprinkled with moments of life-threatening madness."

McNulty chuckled, then winced from the effort. "So we have that in common."

"Like I said, I'm so sorry—"

"It's okay, Diller. It was an accident. Things like this happen."

My mouth fell open. "So you've been shot before?"

McNulty locked eyes with me. "Never."

I cringed again and looked around. "Is there anything I can do for you? Water? Bedpan?"

"Yes." McNulty struggled to sit up. "Quit pretending, Diller. You're no actor."

I felt punched in the gut. "Thanks."

"I'm just being honest. The way I see it, you're like a feral mutt."

"Excuse me?"

"Like the dogs we take in for K-9 school." McNulty took a sip from a cup with a straw in it. "All you need is some discipline and training, and you have the potential to be transformed from a public nuisance to a contributing member of society."

I frowned. "Are you on morphine?"

McNulty laughed. "I got something for you. In that bag on the chair over there."

"Really?" I went over to the chair. The top half of a book peeked out from a paper sack. It read, *Survival Guide.* "What is this?" I asked. "A survival guide for prison?"

"No. Take it out of the bag."

I pulled the book from the sack. The full title read, *Survival Guide for Police Recruits.*

"You ever consider joining the police academy, Diller? A class starts next Tuesday."

"Huh?" I nearly fell on the floor. "What about my police record? Or all those times you arrested me?"

McNulty shrugged. "You were cleared every time. And to be honest, I'd rather have you on *our* side than theirs."

My jaw went slack. "Are you serious?"

McNulty grinned through a wince. "You've definitely got the chops for it. Now beat it, Diller. I need my beauty rest."

"Yes, sir. Get well soon, Sergeant McNutly."

"Mc*Nulty*."

"Sorry." I walked out the door and closed it behind me. Then a thought hit me.

Wait a minute. I have the chops *for it? Did McNulty just insult me?*

I smiled. That had to be a good sign.

Chapter Fifty-Eight

"So you really don't mind going to the Dairy Hog again for lunch?" Brady asked as we pulled into the parking lot of the dive restaurant off Ninth Street.

"No. But I have a confession to make. I think the secret ingredient in their vanilla shakes might be crack."

Brady studied me with all seriousness. "You know, I've suspected the same thing for a while now."

I grinned. "And yet you keep coming back."

"What can I say? It's the crack."

I laughed. "Can you believe McNulty wants me to try out to become a policeman?"

"Absolutely. You're a natural, Doreen."

I frowned. "I am not."

"Sure you are. Stop shooting yourself in the foot."

"Ha ha."

Brady took my hand. "I didn't mean to make a joke. What I mean is, all you lack is confidence. Honestly, I think that's why you didn't make it as an actress."

"Ouch."

"That came out wrong. Doreen, confidence comes from trusting yourself."

"Like you do?"

"Yes. Like *I* do." Brady shot me a grin. "You know, you're already the talk of the police station."

My face flushed. "I am? What are they saying?"

"Mostly jokes. But believe me. Cops only kid you if they like you."

My nose crinkled. "What kind of jokes?"

"Well, nowadays, whenever a suspect gets caught wearing a ridiculous disguise, they call it "Doing a Diller."

"Arrgh!" I groaned. "So what you're saying is that fame finally found me, and that fame is a real butthole."

Brady laughed. "Doreen, whether you choose to be an actress, a cop, or whatever, some nut will always be after your Lucky Charms." He squeezed my hand. "It might as well be me."

• • • •

AFTER A VANILLA-CRACK milkshake and a quick make-out session with Brady, I ditched him for a date with a banana cream cannolo.

"There you are," Aunt Edna said as I came through the door. "Morty's here for dinner, and he brought dessert."

I grinned. "I was hoping he would."

"Which one?" my aunt asked. "Come for dinner, or bring cannoli?"

I hugged her neck. "Both."

"Thanks." She grinned and swatted me on the butt with a dishtowel. "Now go get cleaned up for dinner. I'm making your favorite!"

"Which one?"

She winked. "Both."

• • • •

AS I WAS WASHING UP in the bathroom, I thought I heard my cellphone buzz. I dried my hands and went back to my bedroom. In the pink light of the lava lamp on the bureau, I saw a message blinking on my phone.

I clicked it. An oddly familiar voice waivered over the speaker.

"Doreen? Hi. It's Delores Benny. Are you in town? I have a small part in this movie I'm working on. You'd be my spinster housekeeper. Call me ASAP."

Suddenly, the warm, comforting feeling of my life falling into place here in St. Petersburg felt blasted to pieces by a nuclear bomb called Hollywood.

A decent part? Why now?

Feeling torn, I called the only person who I thought would understand.

"Kerri?" I said into my cellphone.

"Doreen! Hi! How'd the 'insurance video' work out?"

"Perfect. My lifetime policy is locked in. Thank you so much!"

"Glad to hear it. Anytime."

I chewed my bottom lip. "Listen, can I ask you something?"

"Sure."

"I got a call from Hollywood. About a part in a movie."

"Oh. Well, that's good news, isn't it?"

"Two weeks ago, I'd have sold my right kidney for a call like that."

"But not now?" Kerri asked. "What's changed?"

"Everything and nothing. Being a former news anchor, you know what it's like. The biz is completely cutthroat. And even if you make it, you're only as good as your last gig. Being a flop is worse than death. Death you can live down."

"All true," Kerri said. "So what are you asking?"

"Why *now*? Why would the universe send me this role now that my life is ... well, worth living?"

"I'm no guru, Doreen. But I can tell you this. Sometimes things come back to you not to give you a second chance with them, but to remind you of how well you're doing without them."

I burst into tears.

"Are you okay?" Kerri asked.

"Yes. I'm okay. Better than okay. Thank you."

"Anytime."

As I hung up the phone, I suddenly felt more whole, somehow. As if an open wound had finally healed.

I'd come to Hollywood wanting to rewrite showbiz. But as it turned out, I decided to write off Hollywood, instead.

Chapter Fifty-Nine

"Have you been crying?" Kitty asked as I approached the dinner table in the tropical courtyard. Around it, six plates gleamed under the party lights above. I smiled. I was beginning to develop a fondness for even numbers.

"No," I said to the cheerful, pink-clad pensioner with a penchant for poison. "I mean, not *sad* tears, anyway."

"Well, that's good," Aunt Edna said. "Sit down. The veal parmigiana ain't getting any warmer."

I pulled out the last empty chair next to Jackie. "I just got a call from Benny."

Jackie looked around and under the table. "The dog?"

"No. *Dolores* Benny. In Hollywood."

"Oh, the girdle lady," Jackie said. "The one I named Benny after."

"Yes." I snuck a glance at Aunt Edna.

Her face grew taught. "What did she want?"

I shrugged. "Just to say hello."

Relief flooded my aunt's face. When she smiled again, she really *did* look like Elizabeth Taylor. "Dorey, you should've invited Brady to dinner."

I shrugged. "He had to work. *Next* time."

"Good." Aunt Edna smiled at Morty, who looked proud to be sitting by her side. "Tell Brady next time I'll make gingerbread."

"I will." I winked at Morty. "But tonight I'm looking forward to some banana cannoli."

"And you shall have them," he said gallantly. "And afterward, I thought we might have a chat about your mom and dad."

I beamed. "I'd like that."

"You know, *I* could've been an actress," Sophia said, adjusting her Jiffy Pop crown.

"Really?" I asked. "Why weren't you?"

The old Queenpin shrugged her scrawny shoulders. "The sad truth is, there's just not that many roles around for evil geniuses."

"Here, here," I said.

We all laughed and toasted Sophia. "To evil geniuses!"

"You know," Aunt Edna said. "Morty's right, Dorey. When you get that certain expression on your face, you're a dead ringer for Sophia in her early days."

"I knew it!" Sophia said. "You're my granddaughter, aren't you?" She laid down her knife and fork. "That's it. I'm naming my new heir right now!"

Kitty gasped. "You are?"

Sophia's green cat eyes darted from face to face. "I've put this off as long as I can. What we need around here is somebody who hasn't committed the M word yet."

"Murder?" Jackie asked.

"No," Sophia grumbled. "*Medicare*."

"Well, that rules *us* out," Aunt Edna said.

The Queenpin turned her gaze to me. "Young Doreen. You've saved my life twice, now."

I shook my head. "I couldn't have done it without the help of everyone here."

"Maybe not," Sophia said. "But I've been waiting thirty years for someone with enough gumption to blackmail me."

"Seriously?" Kitty said.

Sophia raised a fork in the air like a scepter. "Well done, Doreen. I choose *you* to follow in my footsteps. You want the job?"

I swallowed a dry knot in my throat. A few days ago, I had felt like a total loser with no prospects. But now, in this moment, I felt like a champion with a world of choices laid out before me. I liked this new feeling. I liked this new *me*.

"Um ... I'm honored, Sophia," I said. "Really, I am. But I'm not ready—"

"I'm a reasonable woman," Sophia said, cutting me off. "I know answers aren't always black and white. You don't have to tell me today, Doreen."

"Thank you."

"But don't wait too long," she warned, shooting me a wink. "Someone else might beat you to it."

I nodded. "Fair enough. But, just to be clear, either way, I'm not wearing that turban. Capeesh?"

Laughter burst out around the table. A hopeful giddiness filled the air. As I glanced from face to face, I saw no signs of anger or envy in any of my new found family. Only acceptance. And love.

And maybe a hint of relief.

I drank it in.

This must be what home feels like.

As we ate and drank under the soft yellow lights strung in the courtyard above our heads, I couldn't say what the future held for any of us. The only thing I knew for sure was this:

People are never who you think they are. Especially yourself.

The End

• • • •

THANKS SO MUCH FOR reading ***Almost a Dead Ringer***, the final book in the *Doreen Diller Humorous Mystery Trilogy*.

I hope you enjoyed it, along with the whole series. If so, I'd love it if you would take a few minutes to leave a review. I appreciate every single one! Here's a handy link to the page on Amazon:

https://www.amazon.com/dp/B0BMZCB4S9

Ready for more laughs and twisty mysteries?

Already jonesing for more Doreen Diller and the gang? Well, you never know which of your favorite characters might drop by in my brand new "Val Fremden Strikes Back" series! Click the link below to check out *That Time I Kinda Killed a Guy*, the first book:

https://www.amazon.com/dp/B0C2VZT3LM

Check out my Author Page on Amazon and discover what else I've been up to:

https://www.amazon.com/author/mlashley

While you're there, be sure to follow me so you won't miss out on my next new release or book sale. Thank you so much for being a fan. You totally rock!

More Mysteries by Margaret Lashley

....

FREAKY FLORIDA INVESTIGATIONS

https://www.amazon.com/gp/product/B07RL4G8GZ

Val Fremden Midlife Mysteries

https://www.amazon.com/gp/product/B07FK88WQ3

Val Fremden Strikes Again Mysteries

https://www.amazon.com/dp/B0C2VZT3LM

Doreen Diller Humorous Mystery Trilogy:

https://kdp.amazon.com/en_US/series/W34F3Z8FNY5

Mind's Eye Investigators

https://www.amazon.com/gp/product/B07ZR6NW2N

About the Author

Why do I love underdogs?

Well, it takes one to know one. Like the main characters in my novels, I haven't led a life of wealth or luxury. In fact, as it stands now, I'm set to inherit a half-eaten jar of Cheez Whiz...if my siblings don't beat me to it.

During my illustrious career, I've been a roller-skating waitress, an actuarial assistant, an advertising copywriter, a real estate agent, a house flipper, an organic farmer, and a traveling vagabond/truth seeker. But no matter where I've gone or what I've done, I've always felt like a weirdo.

I've learned a heck of a lot in my life. But getting to know myself has been my greatest journey. Today, I know I'm smart. I'm direct. I'm jaded. I'm hopeful. I'm funny. I'm fierce. I'm a pushover. And I have a laugh that lures strangers over, wanting to join in the fun.

In other words, I'm a jumble of opposing talents and flaws and emotions. And it's all good.

I enjoy underdogs because we've got spunk. And hope. And secrets that drive us to be different from the rest.

So dare to be different. It's the only way to be!

All my best,

Margaret

Made in United States
Orlando, FL
07 August 2023

35865766R00136